41

Shandra Higheagle Mystery Books

Double Duplicity

Tarnished Remains

Deadly Aim

Murderous Secrets

Killer Descent

Reservation Revenge

Yuletide Slaying

Fatal Fall

Haunting Corpse

Artful Murder

Dangerous Dance

D1447969

Homicide Hideaway
Shandra Higheagle Mystery
Book 12

Paty Jager

Windtree Press
Hillsboro, Oregon

This is a work of fiction, Names, characters, places, and incidents either are the product of the author's imagination or are used fictitiously, and any resemblance to actual persons living or dead, business establishments, events, or locales, is entirely coincidental.

HOMICIDE HIDEAWAY

Contact Information: info@windtreepress.com

Windtree Press
Hillsboro, Oregon
http://windtreepress.com

Cover Art by Christina Keerins

Published in the United States of America

ISBN   978-1-947983-84-7

Also available in ebook.

Author's Notes

This book was formulated to introduce to you the main character in my new Gabriel Hawke series. For my hardcore fans this is not the last Shandra and Ryan book. There will be more as long as I can come up with story ideas that I am excited to write.

Special Thanks to:

Lloyd Meeker for his help with aircraft knowledge.

Judy Melinek, M.D.

Crime Scene Writers Yahoo Group

Chapter One

A honeymoon on top of a mountain with no interruptions from Ryan's work sounded like bliss to Shandra. The drive from Nespelem, Washington to Wallowa County, Oregon had taken them the better part of the day. They stopped multiple times along the way, reading historical signs on the sides of the roads. Now they were parked at the small airport between Alder and Prairie Creek.

"Shandra Higheagle Greer," she said out loud, watching Ryan walk over to a man standing beside a small building with an "Office" sign. She was too old to be so giddy over the lyrical way her married name tripped off her tongue. But even though she'd proclaimed she didn't want to marry, Ryan had proved the last three years that she'd known him, that he would never hurt her. She smiled and stepped out of the Jeep as Ryan was greeted by the small man in his seventies.

"Welcome to Prairie Creek Air Field. What can I do for you?" The man shook hands with Ryan.

7

"We're here to fly into Charlie's Hunting Lodge," Ryan said.

"You're early. That flight won't go out until tomorrow mornin." The man tipped his ball cap back and scratched his bald head.

"What do you mean we have to wait until morning?" Ryan asked.

She heard the irritation and tiredness in his tone. They'd married yesterday and had spent the whole night with their wedding guests, leaving Nespelem this morning.

"Ms. Singer won't be able to land at the lodge if she leaves this late in the day." The man shaded his eyes under the ball cap with aviation wings and looked toward what Shandra had learned were the Wallowa Mountains. Land that her ancestors had once called home.

This morning after the last guests celebrating their wedding left her aunt and uncle's ranch, Uncle Martin had explained how Charlie's Hunting Lodge, where they were honeymooning, had been in his family for years. Even when Nez Perce weren't allowed to own land in the Wallowa country. But Charlie Singer's great-grandfather had found a White man willing to pretend he owned the land and run the lodge until the old law was no longer in effect and Nez Perce were allowed back onto the land they had once roamed.

"Is there a place we can spend the night?" she asked.

"The Wagon Wheel is clean and affordable. You should have seen it on the way through Alder," the man said.

Ryan nodded. "I did. Do you have a way to contact

Ms. Singer and let her know we are here?"

The man grinned. "Ask for her when you get a room. She stays at the Wagon Wheel. She flew in earlier today to get supplies and take you out tomorrow." The man tipped his cap back over his eyes and put his hand on the door knob, ending the conversation.

Shandra returned to her Jeep. They'd brought it to save on fuel, not knowing how far they'd have to drive to get to the honeymoon her aunt and uncle had set up.

"At least we'll be able to connect with my cousin tonight and find out what time we'll leave in the morning," Shandra said, climbing into the passenger side.

Ryan slid behind the wheel. "I hope it's not too early. I'm beat."

~*~

At the single story, about a twenty room motel, they walked into the lobby and the middle of an argument. Shandra stopped Ryan, holding him from moving toward the registration desk where a woman in her fifties was as enthralled with the argument as Shandra. People watching was always fascinating.

"Charlie wasn't in his right mind to leave that place to you. Hell, you didn't even come visit him or even know it was there!" shouted a man in his seventies. He was in the face of a woman in her late forties. The woman had on a button-up-the-front, long-sleeved, pink shirt and dress trousers. Her hair was cut short, but stylish.

"I didn't ask for it, but I'll do my best to keep it in the family," the woman said in a tone that knew how to command respect.

"You stole what is mine. Charlie said we were partners. You'll pay. You'll see." The man shoved the woman to the side and wobbled past Shandra and Ryan and out the door.

"Dani, Hector at the airport tried calling you while Doolie was laying into you," the middle-aged woman behind the registration desk said.

The woman, Dani, seemed preoccupied.

Ryan walked up to her. "Are you Dani Singer? The pilot that's taking two people to Charlie's Hunting Lodge tomorrow?"

The woman shook herself and held out her hand. "I am. You must be who Hector was calling about."

"Ryan and Shandra Greer." Ryan shook hands with the woman.

Shandra extended her hand. "My Uncle Martin says we're distant relatives."

Dani scowled. "Really? How?"

Ryan touched Shandra's elbow. "I'm going to get us a room."

"It's ready for you. All you have to do is get the key," Dani said.

"Thanks." Ryan went up to the desk and Shandra remained with Dani.

"Uncle Martin said his uncle on his mother's side was related to Charlie, your uncle. Is your family from the Colville Reservation?"

Dani winced and shook her head. "Charlie and my father were from Lapwai."

Shandra noticed the woman didn't say she was from there. Martin had thought the two young cousins would have something in common because they were both half Nez Perce. It appeared Dani liked to hide that half.

Ryan walked back over. "What time do you want us at the airport in the morning?"

"No later than nine. This time of year, once the air warms up it makes rough currents in the mountains." Dani nodded to them both and strode down the hall of the motel.

"You can tell she's had military training." Ryan hooked his arm through Shandra's and led her down the hall to room 12.

"It's going to be fun getting to know her and understand her feelings about family." Shandra entered the small, but clean, room excited as much about spending uninterrupted time with Ryan as she was about getting to know her cousin.

Chapter Two

The plane banked over a narrow canyon between two mountains. Shandra's fingers dug into the armrest of her seat. The drone of the engine had made it hard to speak the whole trip. Now the sound picked up and the motion leaned Shandra back in the seat as the aircraft's nose pointed upward. The plane tipped forward, barely skimming over several trees and the loud drone of the engine stopped. Had they lost the engine? Her heart crawled up her throat. Stealing a gaze forward, Shandra saw a narrow, short, grassy landing strip. Her cousin didn't seem the least concerned as the plane drifted downward and the sound of air rushed by the small open window on the pilot's side.

Shandra closed her eyes and held her breath.

The plane bobbed a bit to one side and then the other before a small bounce and the drag of the wheels on the turf told her they had landed safely.

"Shandra, we're here," Ryan said, shaking her by the shoulders. "That was some landing," he said to their pilot, Dani.

Opening her eyes, Shandra took in the log building with a porch the length of the front sporting antlers and a sign that read, Charlie's Hunting Lodge. To the right sat three cabins and a long building that she would guess was the bunkhouse. A helicopter was tethered to the ground to the left of the barn and corrals.

"I can see why the only way in is by plane or horse." Shandra unbuckled and ducked to crawl out of the four-seater plane. "The views flying in here were spectacular. It gave me ideas for new vases." She'd brought her sketch pad, knowing even though Ryan wouldn't be able to be contacted here due to no internet or phone service, he wouldn't mind her sketching things that could be incorporated into future pottery projects.

"I wasn't sure you would see any of it the way your eyes were pinched shut at takeoff," Dani said, in a joking tone.

"I've never flown in such a small aircraft." Shandra had been delighted when they'd met little, to no, turbulence today.

"I prefer the small ones over the large planes. The smaller ones are more agile." Dani grabbed their bags which were on top of boxes of supplies. "Go on in. Leslie should have your room ready for you."

Ryan picked up their bags. Shandra slung a backpack over her shoulder as a man she'd judge to be in his sixties came out of the barn headed toward the plane.

The outside of the lodge was rustic almost to the

point of looking about to fall down, but the inside was clean and tidy and showed areas where it had been recently patched.

"It looks like Dani is taking her job of keeping the lodge in the family to heart," Ryan said, nodding toward a ladder and cleaning supplies in the corner of the great room.

A small thin woman with skin that looked as if it had been tanned by cigarette smoke, stepped out of a door to the right. "Are you the newlyweds?"

"Mr. and Mrs. Greer," Ryan said.

Shandra smiled at the way he said the Mrs. with pride.

"You'll be in room one off the great room." She led them into the great room.

Shandra noticed two doors off the larger room. "How many rooms are in the lodge?"

"These two bedrooms are for guests. The hallway to the right of the desk has Ms. Singer's room and the office. My room is off the kitchen through the dining room. It's the door at the end."

"And I saw three cabins? Is the long building a bunkhouse?" Shandra asked, wondering at the woman not being all that sociable.

"Yes. We have the three cabins and the wranglers stay in the bunkhouse." She pivoted and took one step.

"How many wranglers are there?"

"Two when the drunken fool Doolie is here." She didn't wait around for any more questions. Her short legs carried her across the room and through the door before Shandra had stopped wondering at the housekeeper calling Doolie a drunken fool.

"Wasn't Doolie the name of the man arguing with

14

Dani last night?" she asked Ryan as he opened the door to their room.

She lost track of her thoughts catching a glimpse out the window. A majestic snow-capped mountain peak filled the window like a landscape painting. The massive rocks, glittering snow, and towering pines had the appearance of being close enough to reach out and touch. "Look at that view!"

Ryan stood behind her, reaching around and hugging her close. "This is going to be the perfect place for us to spend time together. There's no way the sheriff's department can find me. We can go for horseback rides and day hikes, and spend the nights staring at the stars. He spun her in his arms and kissed her.

Shandra had dreamed of a moment like this ever since they'd both agreed to get married. It had been a decision they both had to agree on as they were both marriage shy. At the wedding, after seeing her family with Ryan's, she knew this would be a lasting marriage and Ryan had proven to her he would never try to change her.

A knock on the door pulled them out of the kiss and her out of her thoughts.

Ryan walked to the door and opened it.

Dani stood back a couple of feet. "I'd like to show you around and then you can make decisions of what you'd like to do while you're here."

"I noticed there's no bathroom connected to the room," Shandra said, having realized there was only one door and that led to the great room.

"Didn't you read the brochure?" Dani asked, the scowl, Shandra was becoming used to seeing on the woman's face, was back. It appeared not knowing everything or following the rules bothered her.

"Uncle Martin handed Ryan the brochure about midnight last night after our wedding and told us where we were going. We didn't really take the time to read it."

"This way." Dani led them down the hall that Leslie had said went to the office and owner's bedroom.

She opened a door and stepped outside. Two small buildings that resembled quaint outhouses stood fifty feet behind the lodge.

"Those are the outhouses. They aren't marked men's or women's, use whichever one is open." Dani turned to the right. A small building with what looked like a water tank on top sat at the corner of the building. "If you don't mind a cool shower, you can take one whenever you wish. I do recommend that to catch the water at its warmest, take a shower just before dark. The water will have had all day to heat up. I'm planning to paint the tank black to gain more use of the sunlight to heat. If you want a warm bath, you'll have to ask Leslie to heat up water you can carry out to the tub and then add water from the shower to make it cool enough."

Shandra glanced at Ryan. He raised his eyebrows and grinned.

"If you were expecting a five-star resort, this isn't it. This is a place where hunters and hikers take a rest and get a meal, and a place where families and retirees come to experience nature." Dani walked around the shower building and over to the cabins. "We have the three cabins. I worked on getting them in shape first. Charlie had let this place go. If I'm going to keep it in the family, it has to make an income. The only way to do that is to fix things so families won't feel like their children could get hurt or catch a disease."

Shandra thought the woman was kidding, but one look at her determined face and she realized Dani believed this place had been a health hazard.

"We saw the ladder and work you've done in the lodge," Ryan commented. He was enjoying watching Shandra try to figure out her cousin. He understood Dani, having been in the military himself and knowing she had gone to the Air Force Academy and been an officer as well as a flying instructor. She knew how to get work out of people and how to push herself. It was admirable, but he wondered if she were lonely. That was something he wouldn't have even thought three years ago when meeting someone. Now that he had Shandra in his life, he understood how lonely he'd been and how she had changed his whole outlook on life.

"The horses can be ridden with or without Clive, my head wrangler. However, these mountains with all their valleys and meadows can start to look alike. If you would like to get back to the lodge without spending a night on the mountain, it would be best to have Clive guide you. At least the first couple of times. He can show you landmarks that will tell you where the lodge is located from your position." Dani stopped at the corrals.

A dozen horses and half a dozen mules stood with their hips cocked in the large corral that looked as if it had been recently rejuvenated. The new yellow poles mixed with the gray older poles looked like something Shandra would draw or put on a vase.

"Do the horses and mules stay up here year

around?" Ryan didn't know much about this area, but from the height of the mountains there had to be deep snow in the winter.

"No. Clive and Doolie will string them down to the trailhead, and they'll be pastured outside of Winslow, one of the towns in the Wallowa Valley. Uncle Charlie has been wintering the stock there for twenty years. I can't see taking that income away from the family that has come to expect it." Dani pushed away from the corral and headed to the bunkhouse.

Shandra nudged Ryan. "I like her. What about you?"

He nodded. There were few people, especially new family members, that Shandra met that she didn't like. Even though the housekeeper had said who stayed in the bunkhouse, Ryan decided to see if he could get Dani to say anything more about the man she was arguing with last night.

"How many wranglers do you have?"

Dani stopped four feet shy of the door on the bunkhouse. "Clive has lived here since Charlie hired him thirty years ago. He's dependable and knows the mountain as well as Charlie did. Then there's Doolie. You met him last night and not in one of his better states." She scowled. "He'd been drinking. He's been drunk ever since I arrived and the lawyer told him I had inherited everything. But the will did state he and Clive could remain here for however long they wanted even if they didn't want to wrangle anymore. I guess Uncle Charlie had told Doolie he was a partner. Which in Doolie's eyes, meant he owned half of this and when Charlie died he owned it all." She sighed and spun away from the building, headed back to the lodge.

"Needless to say, he's been drinking ever since, undependable, and not even showing up at the lodge half the time. When he does, he's unfit to work and just sits around calling me names." She stopped at what appeared to be a footpath through the trees. "This is the one footpath that you can't get lost on if you stay on the trail. It makes a circle and comes out over there behind the corrals. If you want to go for a stroll anytime, you're welcome. Just be aware you are on a mountain and could come across a wild animal. Bear, cougar, wolf. You can usually scare the cougar and wolf away with a shout and waving your arms. Bears, just try to not let them see you and get the hell out of there."

Ryan found it interesting that she hadn't continued talking about Doolie after mentioning he called her names. "What did you do when Doolie called you names?"

Shandra hit him with the back of her hand.

Dani stared at him. "I told him I was sorry Uncle Charlie left the lodge to me. I didn't ask for it, but it's my duty to carry on with it. He was welcome here as long as he showed me respect, otherwise, he would have to find somewhere else to stay."

He wouldn't have thought she'd say anything else given everything he'd witnessed so far. "From seeing him at the motel last night I gather he decided to leave?"

"He did. When I ran into him at the motel, he mentioned he was finding a way to fight the will. I told him it would cost money that he didn't have. All he had to do was be civil to me and he could stay at the lodge. You heard his reply."

Shandra grasped Ryan's hand. "Let's check out the

walking trail."

"You might want to wait until after lunch. It will be set out in thirty minutes. You'll find it through the door to the right when you enter the lodge." Dani strode to the door of the lodge and went inside.

"I guess we could sit on the porch for thirty minutes," Shandra said, leading him over to the long, covered entrance to the lodge.

The building would have been more inviting if there weren't elk and deer antlers hanging from the two-by-four brace across the front of the roof and draped over the railing. It was as if a set of antlers from every animal Charlie and his clients had killed were camouflaging the building and obscuring the view of the mountains on the other side of the canyon.

"Do you think she'll get rid of some of these antlers?" Shandra asked.

Staring at a decades-old elk skull with only a few teeth, he said, "It would be less scary to little kids if she did."

Chapter Three

The trail through the tall pine trees and around huge granite boulders and brush felt like walking through an art gallery. The colors, textures, shadows, and even the scents of pine and new green growth had Shandra's mind flashing with so many vase ideas she had to close her eyes and breathe deeply to settle her thoughts.

"What's wrong?"

"Nothing." The longer she remained in the spot with her eyes closed, the rhythm of the drums from her wedding began to echo in her head. Grandmother flashed in her mind. "What Ella?" she whispered.

A hand touched her arm. She opened her eyes and gazed upon Ryan's concerned face.

"What did you see?"

"Grandmother. She's happy I'm here. We're here." Shandra continued along the trail. Other than Huckleberry Mountain where she lived and dug the clay for her vases, she'd never experienced such a strong sensation of peace and belonging.

She was glad Ryan had insisted she not ignore her visits from her deceased grandmother and believe in the dreams. Shandra held her hand behind her and he grasped it. She had been lucky to find such an understanding man.

They stepped out of the trees and found themselves behind the corrals, just as Dani had said they would.

Ryan stepped up beside her and they started around the corral.

Clive, who they'd met at lunch, hurried out from behind the bunkhouse, loping toward the lodge.

"Come on. Something's wrong." Ryan took off at a jog.

Shandra kept up with him.

They entered the lodge in time to hear Clive say, "Doolie's behind the bunkhouse. I think he's dead."

Dani was on the top of the ladder in overalls. She peered down at the wrangler as if he'd just spouted a foreign language. "What do you mean you think he's dead?"

"He's not movin' or breathin' and he's got blood all over his head." Clive's hands were physically shaking.

"Dani, I'm a detective with the Weippe County Sheriff's Department in Idaho. I'll go take a look. Do you have a way to contact the authorities?" Ryan released Shandra's hand. "Grab my notebook out of my bag."

Shandra nodded.

"If he needs medical aid, I can fly him to La Grande in the helicopter," Dani climbed down the ladder.

Shandra disappeared into the room she and Ryan were staying in and came back with the notepad.

Dani and Ryan were headed out the lodge door.

Shandra followed. They came here to get away from Ryan's work. But she knew her husband. He wouldn't let any wrongdoing go unpunished. He'd get caught up in the investigation. She knew herself well enough to know she would too. This had happened on her cousin's property. Dani would need Ryan's experience and Shandra's help with dreams from her grandmother.

They all went around the end of the bunkhouse where she and Ryan had seen Clive appear. Not five feet from the end was the man Dani had been arguing with the night before. His body sprawled on the ground, his head a bloody mess.

Shandra turned her head from the sight.

Ryan knelt by the man and checked for a pulse. He shook his head. "Call the authorities. This is a homicide."

Dani didn't move, staring at Doolie.

"Dani!" Ryan said loudly, getting her to look at him.

"Yes?"

"Go contact the authorities. This is a homicide. Tell them who I am and that I'm gathering initial information." Ryan stood, putting a hand on Dani's arm and facing her away from the victim. "Go radio or however you contact the outside world."

She nodded and hurried around the end of the bunkhouse.

Shandra studied Ryan. "Does it really look like a

homicide? He didn't just get drunk and fall and hit his head?"

"No accident. This was deliberate. See that stick five feet over there? That has blood and what looks like his long white hair on it. He didn't fall that many times on the same stick." He pointed to the man's head and side of his face.

Shandra nodded. "Do you think Clive did it?"

Ryan studied her. "While we were walking the trail your cousin pointed out to us, he could have been killed. There were only three other people here: Dani, Clive, and Leslie."

Her chest tightened. One of those three had to be the killer. She doubted Dani did it. She was too stunned when she saw the body. But Shandra didn't know her cousin and what she might have been through in the Air Force. Clive had shaking hands. But could that have been because he'd just killed someone or because he was upset and scared? Then there was the cook. She had told them how she felt about Doolie and she had a "don't mess with me" attitude. She would be Shandra's first pick, but she'd learned in all the murders she'd help Ryan solve, that it wasn't always the obvious person.

"Can you go in and get my camera?" He sighed. "I'd hoped to have photos of our honeymoon on it, not a crime scene."

"It's okay. We would have been bored in a couple days anyway." She smiled and kissed his cheek before leaving him to write up his notes.

At the lodge, Leslie and Clive sat in chairs facing the fireplace in the great room. They weren't speaking or looking at one another.

Shandra passed through the room and into her guest room. She rummaged through Ryan's bag and found the camera in a side pocket. A quick glance out the window at the breathtaking view to center herself and she headed out of the room.

Dani entered the main area. "I've contacted the authorities. They said there is a Fish and Wildlife State Trooper up here checking high lakes fisher—"

"That would be Hawke." Clive interrupted. "He's a master tracker and was good friends with your uncle."

"I don't remember meeting anyone named Hawke at the funeral," Dani said, once again scowling.

"I was surprised to see he wasn't there." Clive sat back in the chair as if knowing this Hawke person would take care of things.

"Did they say when he'd arrive?" Shandra asked.

"No. Just that they'd relay the information to him." Dani climbed back up on the ladder.

"What are you doing?" Clive asked.

"Working. He's dead. We can't bring him back, and I have no knowledge of how to investigate his death. I'll leave that to the people that know how. But I do have lots of repairs. So that's what I'll do." Dani glanced pointedly at the two sitting in chairs. "Unless you have skills at investigating a death, I suggest you get back to work as well." She waved a hand at Shandra. "Tell Ryan to let me know if he needs anything."

"I will." Shandra hurried out of the lodge wondering at the angry looks Dani received from her employees. Was it because she'd ordered them back to work or because she was working and acting as if a man hadn't just been murdered on her property?

~*~

Ryan stared down at the stick. It was definitely blood and white hair on the widest end. He left the tree limb laying where he'd found it. The blood would need to dry before he could wrap it in paper to send to a lab. As long as no person or animal came along and touched it, the stick and evidence would be safe.

Shandra came around the end of the bunkhouse. "Do you plan to ask the others what they were doing while we were on our walk?"

He smiled. She had jumped into many investigations since their first encounter where he'd ruled her out as a suspect in a gallery owner's death. "It depends. What did Dani find out?"

"The authorities said there was a Fish and Wildlife Trooper up here somewhere and he'd be contacted to come to the lodge. Clive knows him. Said his name is Hawke and he was good friends with Charlie."

"Is there an ETA on his arrival?" Ryan took the camera and started taking photos. Starting about twenty feet from the body and working his way in a circle toward the victim.

"They didn't know. I guess it depends on how far he is from here when he gets the message. Dani said to let her know if you need her to do anything else." Shandra grinned.

He knew that grin. She'd witnessed something that tickled her. "What has you smiling?"

"Dani is up on the ladder working and told her employees to get back to work unless they have experience in police work."

He smiled and clicked more photos. "That's the military training. You do what you know and leave what you don't know to those who do." Ryan finished his up-close photos and moved over to the murder weapon. He glanced up from the camera. "Keep an eye on everyone and bring me dinner and a heavy coat when it's time. I'm going to have to watch the body until the State Trooper arrives."

"Can't we at least put him in the bunkhouse?" Shandra asked.

"I'd prefer to leave it as is until this Hawke arrives. Some officers can get bent out of shape if their crime scene is messed with, even by other law enforcement."

"Okay. Do you want me to stay with you tonight? I'm sure I could borrow blankets or sleeping bags from Dani." Shandra stood back by the corner of the building.

"We'll see. If the trooper doesn't show up by ten or so, we'll plan to camp out here behind the bunkhouse." Ryan finished his photos. While he had his notepad and camera, he didn't have latex gloves or forensic bags with him. As much as he wanted to check out the man's pockets, it would have to wait.

"Do you mind if I come check on you? Dani, Leslie, and Clive might be the only people we know of here, but there could be someone else who might not want you investigating. I don't like that I can't see you from the lodge." Shandra crossed her arms. A sure sign she wasn't going to take "no" for an answer.

"You may come check on me, but please, keep an eye on the others as well." Ryan walked over to where she stood and kissed her cheek. "I'll be careful."

She nodded and pivoted, walking around the end of the bunkhouse and out of sight.

As much as he hoped it was one of the people here

at the lodge, which would make for a narrow suspect pool, he had to agree with Shandra's logic. It made more sense that someone else on this mountain had killed the man. Which would keep him on the lookout.

Chapter Four

It was 9:30 and there had been no sight of the State Trooper and no communications from anyone to say when he would arrive. Shandra carried two sleeping bags, bottles of water, snacks, and two flashlights out to spend the night with Ryan, watching over the body.

She rounded the corner of the bunkhouse and saw a flashlight bobbing around in the trees beyond the body. From the backlight, she could make out two people. One wore a cowboy hat.

"Ryan!" she called out.

The sound of something running toward her had Shandra shining the light in that direction.

"Dog! No!" a voice she didn't know commanded.

The animal in her beam dropped its haunches to stop, spun around, and raced back toward the two men.

One of the people glanced her direction. "Stay put!" Ryan called.

She set the items she'd carried on the ground and

waited as the light, two men, and the shadow of a dog moved further into the trees to where she could barely see the beam of light. Just as she wondered if she should go back to the lodge where it was warmer, the light grew brighter. Two soft voices conversing murmured through the trees. They walked quicker than when they'd disappeared into the trees.

The two men stopped back at the body. It was easier to see the stranger in the beam of a high-powered flashlight. The man with Ryan had the look of her ancestors. He had distinctive high set cheekbones, duskier skin, regal nose, and dark eyes. His dark hair, under the cowboy hat, brushed the top of his collar. Some gray wisps sparkled in the flashlight beam. He was Ryan's height, broader shoulders, lean, and moved with a fluidity she had noticed in the males of her Colville family.

After discussing the body, Ryan came toward her with his flashlight pointed at the ground.

"State Trooper Hawke showed up about twenty minutes ago. I walked him through what I saw and told him I had photos. We're going to put the body in a tarp and put it in the barn for the night. He's called in a body removal team that will be here late tomorrow. Go back in. I'll be there as soon as we have the body and murder weapon secured in the barn." Ryan leaned over and kissed her temple.

"Why did you walk into the trees?" she asked, picking up the items she'd placed on the ground.

"He noticed traces of someone having walked to the body from the trees. He's going to check it out better tomorrow in the light."

She could tell by Ryan's tone he was impressed

with the other lawman. "Ok. But do come to bed. It is our honeymoon and now that there is another person whose jurisdiction it is, you don't have to be on top of the case."

He grinned. "I'll be in. I promised work wouldn't interfere with our honeymoon."

"Good." Shandra hauled the items she'd thought they'd need for an all-night surveillance back to the lodge.

~*~

Ryan was impressed with Fish and Wildlife State Trooper Hawke. The man had an eye for detail, even in the dark, and had agreed with most of Ryan's findings.

He walked back to the body.

Hawke held out a pair of latex gloves to him. "Don't want to leave any of your DNA on the body."

Ryan shoved his hands into the gloves and watched as the trooper meticulously went over the body, layer by layer, and pulled all the pockets inside out, studying them.

"What are you looking for?" Ryan asked.

"Anything that looks out of place. It is the basis of tracking. Sometimes it's not what you are looking for, but what you don't see, that can tell the truth." Hawke glanced up. "Still have your camera?"

Ryan stuck his hand in his pocket and retrieved the small device.

"Take photos of his pockets." He stood. "I'll get a tarp out of my pack."

Ryan nodded and took photos from several angles. What was he talking about what wasn't there? No money? No receipts?

Hawke returned. "My old friend wasn't a big man.

We should be able to carry him."

As they wrapped the body up in the tarp, Hawke commented, "Why wasn't Charlie with you?"

Ryan studied the man. It was apparent he and the old man who had owned the place were good friends. "Dani and Clive wondered why you weren't at the funeral."

"Funeral?" The man straightened and stared at him. "Charlie is gone?"

"That's what they said." Ryan finished tying the string around the body.

"Why didn't someone tell me? When?" He crossed his arms and glared at Ryan as if he were the one to have left him out in the cold.

"I don't know the answers to any of that. Shandra, my wife, is a distant cousin to Dani, Charlie's niece, that has taken the lodge over. We just arrived today for our honeymoon."

Hawke grunted. "Honeymoon. And you're out here with a body. That must be some wife you have."

"She understands."

"Let's get this body in the barn. I'm going to have a talk with Clive and this, Dani, you say?"

"Yes. Dani Singer."

He humphed and didn't say anything more as they wrapped the murder weapon, placed it on the body, and carried both to the barn.

There was a horse and a mule in the stall next to the body and the dog the trooper had arrived with lay by the stall.

After they placed the body in the empty stall next to the horse and mule, Hawke pointed to the tarp and said, "Guard," to the dog. The animal moved over to the spot and sat at alert.

When Hawke started to walk away, Ryan remained. Someone had to stay with the body.

"Your bride is waiting," Hawke said, when he stopped at the door.

"Someone needs to stay with the body."

"Dog is with the body. No one will get near. Come on." Hawke opened the door and waved for him to follow.

Ryan glanced at the dog, sitting in front of the stall where the body lay. He shook his head and followed the State Trooper. The man knew his dog better than he did.

In the lodge, Dani, Clive, Leslie, and Shandra sat in the great room.

Clive stood and crossed the room, shaking hands with Hawke. "Good to know you're the one they sent."

"Why didn't you tell me about Charlie?" Hawke asked in an accusing tone.

Clive shrunk a bit. "Didn't know how to get a hold of you. I called the state office in Winslow. You were off doing a training somewhere."

Hawke's gaze landed on Dani. "You're the niece that flew planes."

"I fly planes, and I was with the Air Force, yes."

Ryan could practically see the hackles raising on Dani. He decided they needed to get back to the case. "Doolie was arguing with Ms. Singer last night at the Wagon Wheel in Alder," he said.

Dani scowled at him but nodded.

"What about?" Hawke pulled a notebook out of his plaid shirt pocket.

Now that they were inside, Ryan wondered at how

the man was dressed. He looked like any other civilian hiking or packing into the wilderness. He'd removed his cowboy hat as he entered the building, but his cowboy boots had clunked on the wood floor, his jeans were worn, and his plaid shirt didn't show his profession at all. He did have a pistol, not a glock, in a side holster on his belt.

Dani repeated the event that he and Shandra had walked into at the motel.

"I can understand his anger. I heard Charlie tell Doolie many times they were partners." Hawke studied Dani. "I don't remember you ever coming up here."

"I'd never visited before inheriting."

Hawke grunted and turned his attention to Leslie. "No tears for your husband?"

Shandra's head whipped as she stared into Ryan's face. He hadn't known that fact either.

Leslie only glared. "You know there was no love between us anymore. The man was a drunk and worthless."

Dani stared at the woman as well. "You didn't tell me you and Doolie were married."

It appeared the woman had kept the fact a secret from her employer. Why?

"I needed the job. Clive knew I could do it. I've been up here for ten years doing the cooking and cleaning."

Dani huffed. "Maybe cooking but there hadn't been any cleaning done for a long time."

The two women glared at each other.

Ryan noticed one side of Hawke's lips quiver as if he held back a smile.

"Had Doolie been in any arguments other than with

Ms. Singer?" the trooper asked.

The younger woman snapped her glare to Hawke. "I did not kill Doolie. I had no reason to."

"I didn't say you did. I asked if anyone else had been arguing with him." Hawke stared back.

Chapter Five

Shandra couldn't take her gaze from the stare down between Dani and the State Trooper. He had an unorthodox way about him, but she'd liked him from the moment he'd walked in the room and confronted Clive about Charlie. It showed her distant uncle had meant a lot to the officer.

"Doolie thought he was going to inherit this place and had borrowed money thinking that way," Leslie said.

"You mean he'd put this place up as collateral?" Dani asked, irritation ringing in her voice.

"I don't know if he actually did, but he told people he'd be getting this place." Leslie glanced at Hawke. "He owed several people money."

"Then he would have sold the place to pay his debts?" Dani sounded incredulous. "I'm glad Uncle Charlie had enough foresight to not give the lodge to Doolie."

Hawke nodded.

Shandra was glad Hawke and Dani were in agreement about one thing. She slid to the edge of her chair. "But killing him wouldn't have given the people the money he owed them."

It was her turn to feel the dark inquiring gaze of the State Trooper.

"True. But sometimes the people who prey on drunks and druggies decide to do away with them, realizing they will never get paid," Hawke said.

Shandra nodded. Having been involved in nearly a dozen murder investigations with Ryan, she had come to learn there was a dark side in more people than she'd ever expected.

"Where were each of you from one to two this afternoon?" Hawke glanced at Ryan and he nodded.

That was the hour she and Ryan had spent following the path through the trees. The time when they believed Doolie was killed. Shandra had a thought. "It could have been earlier. We were all in the lodge from noon to one having lunch."

"That takes care of the noon hour for all of you. What about after that?" Hawke asked, peering first at Dani.

"After lunch I came in here and resumed patching the corner where the ladder is standing." She pointed to the corner where she had been working when Clive had run into the lodge with Shandra and Ryan following behind him.

"From one until two?" Hawke asked.

"I was here when Clive came in and said he'd found Doolie." Dani glared at the state trooper.

He turned his attention to Leslie. "And you? What

Paty Jager

were you doing from one to two?"

"In the kitchen cleaning up from lunch."

"It takes you an hour to clean up after five people?" Hawke asked.

Her face grew red. "I was also getting things ready for dinner."

"Did you leave the kitchen any time during that hour?"

The cook's gaze flit toward Dani. Why?

"No. I was in the kitchen the whole time." Leslie crossed her arms. A sure sign she was hiding something.

Hawke had written in his notebook as the women had answered his questions. He focused on Clive. "Where were you before you found the body?"

"I left lunch and went to the barn. The family we'd had in here the week before had a little boy that liked to take things apart. I was re-braiding a lead rope he'd unraveled while riding. I'd finished that and decided to go to the bunkhouse. At the end of the building, I thought I heard something moving around behind. Thinking I might get a chance to take care of the skunk that's been coming around, I went to the corner to peek and see if that was what it was before I got my shotgun. Instead of a skunk, I seen Doolie lyin' there on the ground." His face paled at the memory.

"You been having trouble with skunks?" Hawke asked.

Shandra studied the State Trooper. That was all he had to ask from what Clive had said?

"Yeah. They've been visiting behind the bunkhouse at night." Clive didn't seem to think the question was out of the ordinary.

Hawke faced her. "Mrs. Greer, I understand you were walking the back trail with your husband before the body was found."

"Yes. We set out right after lunch. When we walked by the corrals, we saw Clive come from behind the bunkhouse and hurry to the lodge." She smiled, hoping to lighten the man's disposition.

He jotted that information down and looked up. "When you first saw the body, what did you think?"

Why was he asking her that? "That he was dead."

"Was that before your husband said he was dead?"

"Yes."

"Did you think he'd been dead a while or it just happened?"

She shook her head. "I'm not an expert—"

"I know. What did you see?"

She closed her eyes and conjured up the image of Doolie on the ground. "The top of his head, bloody, but not oozing." She opened her eyes. "The blood was dry, crusty."

"That means Clive couldn't have just killed him." Hawke looked at the wrangler. "Unless he'd killed him that morning and went back there to make it look like it had just happened."

"I didn't harm a hair on Doolie's head," Clive said, leaning forward in the chair. "He might have hit the bottle hard after Charlie's death, but he never did anything to me to make me want to kill him."

Leslie stood and pointed a finger. "You accused him of stealing from you just last week."

Clive's face darkened as he glared at the woman.

Shandra glanced at Ryan and then Hawke to see if either were going to step between the wrangler and cook staring daggers at one another.

"What did he steal?" Hawke finally asked.

"The shotgun my granddaddy gave me when I was twelve." The anger in Clive's voice startled Shandra. He'd seemed like a pretty mellow man up until now.

"Why did he steal it?" Ryan asked, and received a glare from the state trooper.

"He owed people money," Clive said.

Dani stood up. "Has he stolen items from here? From the lodge?" She stopped in front of Clive and peered down at him.

The wrangler shrugged. "Don't know. I only know my shotgun came up missing after he'd gone to town the last time."

"When Dani told him to leave?" Shandra asked and caught one of Hawke's glares as well.

She was happy to see he wasn't telling her or Ryan to stand down and let him do the questioning, but she could see their butting in upset him.

"Ms. Singer, sit down," Hawke said.

The woman spun on her heel and scowled at him. "I have a right to know if there are items missing from the lodge."

Hawke waved a large hand. "You can assess the situation in the morning. With the thief dead, nothing more will go missing."

Dani crossed her arms and sat back in the chair she'd vacated.

The State Trooper peered at Shandra again. "What else did you see?" He glared at everyone else. "And the rest of you keep quiet until I ask you a question."

It was apparent the officer didn't like to be interrupted.

"He lay on his front, his face in the grass. His arms were at his side. He didn't stop the fall. His clothes had mud, his boots appeared dark, like they were wet." She shook her head. "That's all I can remember."

Hawke nodded. "How did he leave the mountain?" he asked Clive.

The man's face grew red again. "He took the black mule, Spade."

Dani shot to her feet once more, her face a contortion of rage. "You let him take one of the animals? We need those and he had no right to it."

Clive shrunk back in the chair, away from the angry woman. "I figured he didn't get the lodge like he'd been talking about, he might as well have an animal he could sell."

Dani threw her arms in the air and strode over to the granite fireplace. She slammed a fist on the shiny worn mantle and muttered something.

Shandra crossed the room to her cousin. "I'm sorry."

Dani shook her head and squeezed the bridge of her nose. "It's not your fault. It's mine for not finding new help. An officer knows that to clean up a shoddy department, you throw out the baggage and start fresh. That damn will that made me responsible for this place and the people has been a down draft since I received the letter."

Shandra remained at Dani's side until a yawn reminded her it had been a long day without sleep the night before. Hawke and Ryan had convened at the far side of the room. She assumed they were comparing notes.

"You may all go to bed. I'll be bunking in the barn

with the body." Hawke walked over to Dani. "Let me know when you hear what time the retrieval team will arrive."

She gave a curt nod.

Ryan grasped Shandra's hand. "Let's go to bed."

She followed him to their room. Once inside she turned to him. "What were you and Hawke talking about?"

Ryan began undressing. "While the two employees seem the most logical to have committed the crime, we can't rule out that someone followed him back up the mountain and killed him."

"Is that what you and Hawke were doing when I came to sit with you? You saw tracks?"

"He spotted indentions of more than one set of footprints. He wants me to keep an eye on the body in the morning while he follows the tracks." Ryan climbed into bed and patted the mattress beside him. "You going to join me?"

She smiled, undressed, turned out the light and settled into the bed and Ryan's arms.

~*~

Shandra rode a mule through the forest. She knew it was a mule because of his long ears. How did she get here? The pine trees, a boulder, they looked familiar, but she didn't know why. Dismounting by the boulder, she spotted something shiny. Two old pistols, a breast plate made of elk bone. How she knew this, she wasn't sure. "Ella, are you seeing this?" she asked. Shandra opened a box the size of one of her larger vases and discovered small bags of gold dust.

Motion as if an earthquake were shaking the boulder, startled her.

42

Drifting out of the dream, Shandra realized the rocking motion was the bed. She rolled and found Ryan sitting on the edge of the bed, looking out the window.

Shandra slipped up behind him. "I think Doolie stole more than Clive's shotgun."

Chapter Six

Ryan carried a plate of food out to the barn. He figured it was the least he could do for State Trooper Hawke before he trailed after the tracks they'd discovered last night. Dispatch had radioed fifteen minutes earlier that the recovery team had headed out at first light. He wasn't sure what time that would have been at the base of the mountain. Up here it had been five-thirty.

He opened the barn door and found Hawke propped up against the end of the stall, his hat tipped over his face.

The dog raised his head, sniffing.

Not sure if the animal was catching his scent from last night or the bacon on the plate, Ryan approached slowly. "Good dog. You know me."

The animal stood, stretched, and bared his teeth as Ryan moved toward Hawke.

A low rumble in the animal's throat popped the

State Trooper's hat up and his eyelids opened.

"Down, Dog," Hawke commanded.

The mutt plopped down on his butt but continued to stare at Ryan.

"Brought you some breakfast and news," Ryan said, handing the tray of food down to Hawke.

"Good news? You found the killer?" The man chuckled under his breath.

A joker it seemed. He'd been professional last night. "Not the killer. Dispatch said the retrieval party left at daylight."

Hawke picked up the travel cup of coffee and sipped. He nodded his head. "They'll be here about noon then."

"Do you still plan to follow those tracks?" Ryan asked.

The State Trooper nodded and bit into the bacon. He wasn't one for many words.

Ryan wasn't sure how to tell the man about Shandra's dream. He had a feeling Doolie had been taking items from the lodge and hiding them. He could have been on his way back to get more when whoever it was ended his life.

Hawke peered up at him. "You're either constipated or have a question."

The statement caught him off guard. "Neither." Ryan took a seat on a bale of hay. "In case you didn't figure it out, Shandra is half Nez Perce."

The man nodded his head. "She is intuitive."

"Yes, that, and she has dreams. Last night she dreamt she was riding a mule and discovered a cache of items. Things she thinks may have come from the lodge." He studied Hawke. Ryan had to give the man

45

credit, he didn't look at him as if he were crazy.

"I see. Why does she think the items came from the lodge?" He scooped the over-easy eggs into his mouth with a slice of toast while watching Ryan.

"A feeling. Shandra has never been here before, so she would have no idea if the items were from the lodge. But she believes they are. And that you could find them when you retrace the footsteps of Doolie or his killer."

The plate was empty of food. Hawke tipped the cup of coffee and gulped it down. He wiped his mouth on a bandana he'd pulled out of a pocket, and stood, handing the tray to Ryan. "I'll see what I find when I follow the tracks." He walked over to a horse in a stall, patted it on the forehead, and hooked a lead rope to the halter.

"Take those in the house. When you return, I'll be ready to leave." Hawke turned his back to Ryan and began saddling his horse.

Ryan returned the tray to the house, grabbed a travel cup of coffee, and found Shandra waiting for him by the door.

"You don't have to sit with me," he said.

"This is our honeymoon. I want to be where you are." She opened the door and they walked to the barn.

Hawke had a canvas saddlebag across the rump of his horse and a scabbard with the butt of a rifle sticking out.

Ryan asked the question he'd been wondering about since the man walked up to him last night. "Are you up here on vacation?"

"No. I'm working. The high lakes are prime fishing right now and people like to take the fish without a license. This is also the time of year the cartels start setting up marijuana grows."

"Why are you out of uniform?"

Hawke glanced down at his attire and back at the detective. While the county detective had been competent with his information and questions he'd asked the people of the lodge, Detective Greer seemed a bit uptight for a man on his honeymoon. "Wandering around up here with a uniform on would be like wearing a target. This way, the fishermen and the cartels don't know I'm a State Trooper and anyone else doing illegal activities won't take a pot shot at me."

"Makes sense," Shandra, the man's wife, said.

She had impressed him from the first moment he'd encountered her. Knowing she dreamed events that could have happened and that her husband believed in them, she'd gained even more of his respect.

"If I'm not back before they retrieve the body, tell them everything that I've found out so far." He started across the area between the barn and bunkhouse and whistled to Dog.

"Will you be back by dark?" Shandra asked.

"It depends on the tracks." He touched his hat brim and led Jack to the back of the bunkhouse.

He did another look around to see if there had been a skunk coming around as Clive had said or if the sounds may have been made by a larger animal, one with two legs, a penchant to steal, and smoke marijuana.

The area didn't hold any lingering aroma from a skunk. A good whiff, though, did have the iron tang of blood. He was surprised that the carnivores of the forest hadn't followed the scent. The only skunk track he found was old.

Daylight made it easier to check out the bushes, rocks, and trees for any sign of a fight or the assailant hiding.

It appeared Doolie had been back here for whatever reason and the person walked up behind him and hit him with the limb, not just once but multiple times. That seemed like anger more than just trying to kill someone. But he'd keep those thoughts to himself. His superior only wanted the details.

Satisfied he'd seen everything there was to see in this area, he followed the direction of the bent grass marking the trail of Doolie and his possible killer.

Chapter Seven

Shandra sat beside Ryan on a hay bale at the entrance to the barn. He'd made sure there was no other way someone could get into the building and placed the bale out in the sunshine.

"Did you tell Trooper Hawke about my dream?" she asked, hoping it helped but not wanting the man to think she was a crazy person.

"I did. It didn't seem to shock him. He took it in and then went on his way." Ryan stared at the top of his coffee cup. "He seems very thorough but almost nonchalant about this murder." He shook his head. "I can't place it."

"I didn't think he was nonchalant. He was boring holes in Dani last night and didn't take it any easier on the two people he knows." Shandra had thought the Trooper was tough but fair-minded.

"This morning he made a couple of comments that…" He snapped his fingers. "They were like something my friend Rodney would have said."

"Rodney, your Blackfoot friend?" Shandra asked.

"Yes. The same type of humor. I was expecting the same attitude he'd shown last night and that's why it threw me off." Ryan took a sip of coffee.

"It's good to know he's not so stern as he showed last night." Shandra stared at the lodge. "Do you think Leslie or Clive killed Doolie?"

"I don't know. But it's not my job. Once this body is out of here, I want to get back to our honeymoon. Horseback rides and moonlight walks." He picked up her hand and kissed her knuckles. "No more talk of any of this. Hawke is in charge."

She nodded, but knew that wasn't going to happen. With grandmother coming to her last night, they were going to be up to their eyeballs in the whole thing.

A man with a backpack walked out of the woods almost directly in front of the lodge. His beard was about an inch long, brown with some copper highlights. He appeared tall and lithe, carrying a rather bulky pack. He was dressed in dirty muddy jeans, T-shirt, and hiking boots.

He was headed straight for the lodge. When he disappeared into the building, Shandra stood. "I'm going to go see who that is."

"You know hikers and hunters use the lodge as a stopping place all the time," Ryan said.

"I know. But I'm interested in anyone who would be hiking up here. He could have seen something." Shandra took one step and Ryan caught her hand.

"Don't ask him any questions. And make sure no one says anything about the body." Ryan's voice was laced with authority.

"He'll find out when the retrieval team arrives," she countered.

"He doesn't need to find out anything if he stops in and leaves before they get here."

She nodded and strode over to the lodge. Stepping through the door, she heard Dani greeting the hiker.

"Hello, I'm Dani Singer, the owner of the lodge."

"Harris Rusk. I've been up here hiking about a week. Before I headed up the mountain someone had mentioned there was a lodge where a hiker could get a good meal and possibly a shower."

Shandra stopped inside the door, watching the man. He and Dani shook hands.

"Yes, we serve breakfast, lunch, and dinner and the shower is this way." Dani led him down the hallway to the back of the building.

Shandra followed behind, noticing the man glanced into the open doors of the office and Dani's room. She stopped at the back stoop and watched Dani open the shower building and show the hiker the facilities.

"Because you aren't a guest staying here, you'll have to use your own towel," Dani said before closing the door on the man. She looked up, spotted Shandra, and scowled.

Dani hurried over to the door. "What are you doing? Spying on me?"

"Not you. The hiker." Shandra didn't feel the need to say anything different. "Ryan wants to make sure no one tells him about the body in the barn."

Dani scowled at her again. "That's a given. Why would I announce that fact to anyone visiting?"

"Make sure Leslie knows that, too." Shandra stared at the shower house as if it would give her information about the man.

"I'm sure he'll be here for lunch, since he mentioned a meal. Clive said that's when the retrieval team will arrive. I told Leslie to make sure there is enough food for everyone." Dani glanced at the shower house. "How do I explain them to Mr. Rusk?"

"We'll let the people who come do that." Shandra pivoted and walked back into the lodge. She took a seat in a chair in the great room where she could keep an eye on anyone coming into the lodge through the back door.

Dani noticed. "Are you going to spy on everyone who stops in while you're here?"

"No. I'm just curious about a man who shows up the day after we find a body." She raised an eyebrow. "You might want to make sure the doors to the office and your room are closed." She made the motion of turning a key. "Tight."

Dani huffed but she hurried back down the hall and returned within minutes. She took her place up on the ladder in the corner of the great hall.

Shandra wondered what Dani was doing in that corner that was taking her so long to fix.

Twenty minutes later, the hiker appeared in a clean T-shirt and jeans, his feet were bare and he carried his boots. He was either being overly careful to not put dirt in a hunting lodge or he'd sneaked in the back hoping to check out the back rooms and discovered them locked.

~*~

Hawke had followed the trail of two sets of prints for a mile, when they split. Making it apparent Doolie had known his attacker and they had met here for a reason.

At first, he'd believed Doolie was leading someone, but he realized the man had followed Doolie. Why he wasn't sure.

He took time to scour the ground, looking for any signs to explain why they'd met up. A breeze fluttered across his cheek. The branches of the trees moved and sunlight glinted off something. Keeping his gaze on the area, he moved closer.

"Dog, stay," Hawke said, hearing the animal moving through the brush toward him.

On his knees, he parted the grass and plants. A whiskey bottle had been flung to the side. Hawke pulled a latex glove out of his pocket and picked the bottle up with a finger in the opening.

Back at Jack, he unbuckled the saddlebag one-handed and pulled out an evidence bag. He wrote the time and date on the bag and then took a photo of the area where he'd found the bottle. Also, photos of the few visible foot prints.

He still didn't have an answer to why the two had met here and the other man had followed.

If this man had followed and killed Doolie, where were his tracks leaving the crime scene? This puzzled him. The set of prints he'd followed to here, only came from this direction. There were none that came back this way. Had he missed a set at the crime scene?

Shoving the bagged bottle into the saddlebag, he swung up on Jack and whistled for Dog. There had to be a set of prints leaving the area other than those of the people who found the body and used the same route to and from the scene.

Chapter Eight

Ryan stood as several horses came out of the trees and walked across the grassy runway. There were three people on horses, the lead person led a mule with a packsaddle.

Hawke had returned an hour earlier. After placing an evidence bag beside the body, he and the dog disappeared on foot behind the bunkhouse.

Clive came out of the bunkhouse as the horses stopped at the corrals.

"Hello, Clive," the lead man, dressed in civilian clothes, said.

"Howdy, Bob." The wrangler grabbed the reins of the woman's horse. "Dr. Vance. Sorry you had to make the trip up here on horseback."

"That makes two of us," the woman responded, dismounting stiffly.

The other man dismounted and tied the reins of his horse to the corral beside the others.

Clive led the small group over. "This here is Ryan Greer. He's a detective from Idaho who is stayin' here."

Ryan held out his hand and shook with each person.

"Fish and Wildlife State Trooper Bob Sullens," the one who led them into the area said as he shook.

"Detective State Trooper Tad Ullman," the other man said.

"Dr. Gwendolyn Vance. Medical Examiner for Wallowa County."

Ryan opened the barn doors to allow more light inside. "Clive found the body of a male Caucasian…" He went on to tell them everything they'd discovered.

"Hawke around?" Ullman asked.

"He came back from following some tracks this morning and disappeared shortly after returning." Ryan pointed to the bunkhouse. "He disappeared behind there. That's where the body was found."

Ullman nodded and headed that direction.

Dr. Vance did a short examination of the body and the murder weapon. "I concur with this gentleman and Hawke. The limb was used to bludgeon this man to death."

Sullen nodded. "You said you took photos?"

"I did. Hawke also took photos," Ryan added.

"We'll need your SD card." Sullen walked out of the barn and came back with a body bag.

"After I help you here, I can get the card out of my camera. It's in the lodge." He went on to explain that he and Shandra were on their honeymoon.

"Heck of a way to spend your honeymoon," Sullen said.

Ullman walked into the barn. "No sign of Hawke. He must have found another trail to follow."

The two men talked about the other trooper with respect.

They had the body in the bag when Shandra entered the barn.

"You'll have to leave," Ullman said, pulling his badge out from under his shirt by the chain around his neck.

Ryan moved to Shandra's side. "This is my wife. She saw the body and has been keeping me company while I've guarded it."

"I came out to tell you, lunch is ready in the lodge." She smiled at each of the retrieval members, tucking an arm around his waist.

"That sounds good to me. I didn't have enough time to get more than a piece of toast and coffee before meeting up with these two," Dr. Vance said, walking toward the door.

Ryan stopped them. "A hiker came in this morning. He doesn't know anything about this body."

The others nodded.

"He took a shower and is staying for lunch, though I saw him visiting with Dani a few minutes ago and it looked like they were headed to the room next to ours." Shandra raised one eyebrow.

Ryan understood her hesitancy to have the man in the house, considering they were trying to investigate who had killed Doolie.

"We'll just be horseback riders going through," Sullen said.

"Until he sees the body bag on the mule when you leave," Ryan added.

The trooper shrugged. "He'll have to wonder then, won't he?"

Ullman offered to remain with the body while the others went in for lunch.

In the dining room off the kitchen, Ryan got his first good look at the hiker. He appeared to be making himself at home. He had on flip flops and was talking with Clive about the availability of going for a horseback ride that afternoon.

The hiker's attention landed on Sullen, Dr. Vance, and Ryan when they moved to sit at the table.

Dani passed the bread and plate of meats and cheese to the hiker. "Mr. Rusk, this is Ryan, Shandra's husband."

Ryan nodded. The hiker glanced at Shandra and back at him and nodded.

"And it looks like we've had a few more unexpected guests," Dani said, leaving it open for the trooper and doctor to introduce themselves.

"We were riding by and saw the lodge. Doc-Darlene, remembered something about the lodge serving food," Sullen said, taking the plate as it was handed to him.

"We're pleased you could join us," Dani said with a little too much emphasis on 'pleased.'

Ryan made his sandwich and peered across the table at the hiker. "Where have you been on the mountain? Any place that Shandra and I might want to visit?"

"I started out a week ago from Minam and worked my way this way. I saw a lot of beautiful country, but I can't think of one place that was more spectacular than another." The man took a bite and chewed, ending the conversation.

Shandra tapped Ryan's foot with hers. He glanced her way, and she nodded toward the dining room window, facing the back of the lodge. Hawke was striding past the shower house.

"Excuse me." Ryan stepped over the bench and headed down the hall to the back door to intercept Hawke and tell him about the stranger before he walked in and said something.

Hawke stopped at the open door. "I see the retrieval team arrived. I figured they'd be in here and you'd still be in the barn."

"Ullman is with the body." Ryan put up a hand when Hawke started to go around him. "A hiker arrived here this morning. Looks like he plans to stay a night or two."

Hawke stared at him. "And?"

"We haven't said anything to him about the body and the two in eating didn't say who they were." Ryan glanced toward the barn.

"Why are we pussyfooting around this hiker?" Hawke asked.

"Just thought it wouldn't be a good image for the lodge if word got out there had been a murder here."

"Doolie could have died of a natural cause," Hawke said. "Then it wouldn't matter that there is a retrieval team here."

"But he didn't, and everyone on this mountain is a suspect," Ryan said, returning his gaze to the State Trooper.

"True. I need to report my findings to Ullman. Why don't you bring us some lunch?" Hawke pivoted, strode down the steps, and over to the barn.

Ryan shook his head and returned to the dining room. He picked up a clean plate and put meat, cheese and bread on it and grabbed two full glasses of iced tea.

No one said anything as he left, but he felt the

hiker's gaze on him.

"What do you do for a living?" Rusk asked as Ryan left the room.

Shandra set her gaze on the man who had tried to keep her out of the barn earlier. What would he say?

"I work for Fish and Wildlife." The trooper took a bite of his sandwich.

Rusk turned his attention to the woman. "And you?"

"I'm a doctor." She sipped her iced tea.

The hiker studied them both and continued to eat.

Shandra felt a need to break the silence. "Dani, is there a horse trail Ryan and I can take this afternoon that will get us back here by dinner time?"

"You'll have to ask Clive. I've only been here for a few months and have spent all my time fixing the place up. I haven't had a chance to check out the trails." Dani motioned to the wrangler.

"There's a couple good ones that will only keep us out for a few hours. They're good for people who don't ride much," Clive said, his gaze straying to the hiker.

"That's not me. I ride my horses on my mountain every chance I get. This time of year, it's every day," Shandra said.

Dani asked her about "her mountain" and Shandra explained how she owned property on Huckleberry Mountain in Idaho. How she used the clay to make vases and had a woman who lived in the barn and helped with the animals and her clay. She started to tell about a workshop she would teach this fall when Ryan returned from the barn.

As if it was a cue, Sullen and the doctor rose.

"Thank you for the lunch. Hawke will square things up with you," Sullen said, nodding to everyone and walking out of the dining room with the woman.

"Who is this Hawke?" Rusk asked.

"Another visitor," Ryan said.

Shandra turned to Ryan. "Clive has a ride for us to go on this afternoon."

"Good. I could use a ride." Ryan grasped her hand and gave it a squeeze.

Something was up. She didn't know what, but she could tell by the way he looked and squeezed her hand he had something to tell her.

Chapter Nine

"I'd like to go for a ride this afternoon, too," the hiker said.

Ryan stared at the intruder. He'd shown up right after they'd found a body. Now the man was horning in on his afternoon with Shandra. To say anything would be rude, but he didn't like the man and didn't want him invading their time together.

"I'll saddle up four horses," Clive said. He rose and left the room.

Ryan grasped Shandra's hand and stood. "Let's get ready."

She studied him as he led her out of the dining room and into their room.

Once the door was closed, he paced the floor.

"What's wrong?" Shandra asked.

"I don't like having that hiker here or going with us on the ride." He stopped and stared out the window. "There's something about him... I don't know what it is, but I don't trust him."

"Neither do I. That's why his going on the ride with us is good." Shandra told him how she thought he was casing the place his first trip through the house. "I don't like the idea of him being here with just Dani and Leslie."

He had to agree with that. "Then I guess it's a good thing he's going with us."

Shandra pulled out a pair of cowgirl boots from her bag.

"I should have known you'd have a pair of riding boots." He had on his boots. It was rare he wore anything else.

She smiled, slipped off her shoes, changed her socks, and shoved her feet into her boots.

Shandra tied a light sweatshirt around her waist and smiled. "Let's go. I'm ready to see more of this mountain."

He felt the same. Being cooped up with the body as much as he had, he was ready to be free of his job.

~*~

Ryan left Shandra sitting in the great room to go out and help Clive. The wrangler was saddling four horses by the bunkhouse. Shandra closed the front door to the lodge as the retrieval team led the mule with the body bag out of the barn. Shandra turned from the door and walked over to a chair, watching the hiker. He was too curious.

"What were those two people really doing here?" he asked.

"I don't know. Probably the same as you. Heard the lodge served meals and stopped in for something different than they were packing." She picked up a magazine, trying to prevent any further questions.

"Why did your husband take food outside?" He stood by the mantel, running a finger over an old wind up clock.

"I don't know. That's something you'll have to ask him. Why did you decide to stay at the lodge? Doesn't that defeat the purpose of backpacking in the mountains?" She decided to turn the tables and ask him questions.

He stood in front of a painting of a brave on a horse that hung over the couch. His face turned toward the dining room and back. If she hadn't been watching him close, she wouldn't have seen the movement. What about the dining room and kitchen made him check there before answering her?

"I was tired of camping." He moved on to the wall adorned with a hatchet, headdress, peace pipe, and breastplate.

"We're ready," Ryan said, entering the lodge.

Shandra hurried over to her husband and whispered. "He's been looking everything over and asking questions about you and the others."

Ryan shrugged and whispered, "They're gone." Then he spoke in a normal tone to Rusk, "If you're riding this afternoon, you need to get a move on."

Shandra walked out the door and strode over to where Clive held the four horses.

"You can ride Queen. She's one of the new horses Charlie bought the spring before last." He held out the reins to a black horse with a white spot on her forehead that resembled a crown.

"I'd be delighted to ride Queen. Any habits I should know of?" She slipped the reins around the mare's neck and stepped into the stirrup, swinging her leg over the horse's rump and to the other side.

"She likes to pretend she's scratching at a bug biting her leg, but she's really looking for a bite of grass." Clive grinned.

"Gotcha. Don't let her stop and scratch too often." She patted the mare's neck.

"This one's for you," Clive held out the reins of a gelding, who looked half asleep, to Rusk.

The hiker took the reins and pulled himself up onto the saddle.

Ryan grabbed the reins of another gelding and swung up on its back. Clive took the lead with Rusk behind him. Shandra followed the stranger and Ryan brought up the rear.

Shandra always enjoyed horseback rides on Huckleberry Mountain, but this mountain had just as much appeal to her. They took a westerly route away from the buildings and through the trees. She was in awe of the huge pine trees, the massive granite boulders, and the pristine snow-topped mountain peaks.

Clive turned in his saddle and said, "This route generally only takes about three hours, but we'll hit one of the highest spots in the area. It's a great view."

"That sounds good." Shandra smiled at the man. He'd been trying hard to make sure she and Ryan had a good time while they were here. It was easy to see why he'd had his job of wrangler at the hunting lodge for so long.

Ryan rode his horse up alongside hers when the trail widened. "This is beautiful country. I can see why it was hard for the Nez Perce to give up."

Shandra studied Ryan. He never ceased to amaze her

with his compassion even though his job made him cynical.

They came to an outcropping over a deep valley below. Clive dismounted and waved his arms. "This is the Minam Canyon. Hunters have enjoyed good hunting in this canyon and mountain for years. The hikers enjoy not only the ruggedness but the view and solitude. I think this is the best area in the Wallowa Whitman National Forest."

Shandra and Ryan dismounted and walked over to stand beside Clive. The view was spectacular. She peered down onto the various green tops of trees. Small creeks, filled with the spring runoff from the snowy mountain peaks, followed cracks between the rocks and disappeared under the canopy of trees and bushes. Small dots that had to be wildlife moved about below. The air was crisp and fresh. It was like being on top of the world.

"I've never seen anything so spectacular." Shandra stared in awe.

"This is why I hung out here for thirty years as the wrangler at Charlie's lodge. I can't think of any better place in the world to be," Clive said.

Shandra gazed at the man. Tears glimmered in his eyes. "Are you going to stay on with Dani?"

The man shook his head. "I don't know. I'm not partial to change. And she's got all kinds of ideas for the lodge."

"What kind of changes?" Rusk asked.

Shandra jumped from the sound of his voice. He hadn't dismounted and joined them. She'd forgotten he was there.

"She's planning to put this out on the Internet. Make

65

it accessible to families and business groups. I just don't know if I can handle all that." Clive wrapped the reins around his hands. "It just doesn't feel right. All those years Charlie talking about him and Doolie as partners, that I'd always have a place to live. It just seems wrong that he gone and give it to her."

Rusk looked interested, when he should have been bored or confused.

Shandra switched her attention to Clive. Was he as opposed to Dani taking over the lodge as Doolie had been? "Well, you know, maybe as he got older he realized it would take somebody who knew how to fly an airplane to get people in and out of here," Shandra said.

"I understand that." Clive tipped his hat back and scratched his head. "Neither Doolie nor I know how to fly one of them contraptions. It just seems like we could have hired somebody."

"I read in the brochure this lodge has been in the family for centuries. Doesn't it make more sense that it stays with a family member?" Ryan asked.

"Dani is a relative of Charlie, the original owner?" Rusk asked.

Shandra decided to call his bluff. "Did you know Charlie?"

The man's eyes peered straight at her. "I met him once down at the Blue Elk. That's how I knew about this place."

She glanced over at Clive. He looked skeptical. She wondered if Charlie had even frequented the Blue Elk, whatever it was.

Clive shifted his attention back to Ryan. "Yeah, I understand him wanting to keep it in the family. It's a sense of pride, bein's how they owned it even when the government said they couldn't have any land in the area. I'm thinking though, that Charlie thought she'd just keep it in the family by name and let me and Doolie run it. But she is all about running the whole thing and making a profit, and bringing in all these other people. She's just changing everything."

"She's just trying to make it profitable for not only her but everyone who works here," Shandra said. She understood her cousin's desire to make the lodge profitable. There were other family members who, down the road, one day, would inherent the lodge from her. If not her children, then her nieces or nephews. Dani wanted to make sure it was a viable way to make a living.

Clive mounted his horse. "Come on. There's more trail to see."

Shandra swung up on her horse at the same time as Ryan. They waited for Rusk to follow Clive before falling in line behind him. They continued through more timber, brush, and beautiful scenery.

The forest opened and a meadow filled with wild flowers spread out before them. Shandra exclaimed, "Please stop, Clive!" She was off her horse and taking pictures before Clive brought his horse and Rusk's to a stop. She had never seen a more beautiful sight than the wash of colors bobbing in the slight breeze along with swaying bright green meadow grass. The floral scents, enhanced by the sunlight, added to the earthy scents she'd been smelling.

She crouched to get a different shot of the flowers and a doe walked to the edge of the meadow. Shandra stood to take its photo, but the deer spun around, diving back into the safety of the trees. She hoped the photos she took of the animal in motion would turn out.

Rusk sat atop his horse, swatting at bugs.

Shandra walked over to where Ryan held her horse and nodded toward the man who was definitely showing he wasn't a person used to being on the mountains. She and Ryan had applied bug repellent before they left the lodge. If Rusk were really a hiker, he would have done the same.

"Done taking photos?" Clive asked.

"Yes. Thank you for stopping." Shandra remounted her horse.

Clive nodded and continued on through the meadow. The sound of a small creek could be heard before they came upon it. The horses walked through the ankle-deep clear water without hesitating.

As if he needed to fill the silence, Clive began to tell stories that captured the experiences of people that had visited the lodge.

The stories, the motion of the horse beneath her, and taking in all the scenery made this ride even better than she'd hoped. A scan up the mountainside to her right revealed an open patch in the trees. She recognized the sight. Her heart stuttered to a stop before starting up again. It was the tree and the boulder in her dream.

"Ryan!" Shandra pulled back on the reins, waiting for Ryan to come abreast of her.

Ryan arrived at her side, worry furrowing his brow. "What's wrong?"

Shandra pointed to the clearing between the trees and the granite boulder beyond. "That's the boulder that was in my dream. The one that had the items."

Ryan glanced at the clearing then up at the two

horses in front of them. Rusk looked back at them at that moment. Ryan nudged his horse forward. "Keep moving. We'll have to come back here tomorrow and see what we find."

Shandra nodded, taking one last long look at the area to make sure she had a good impression of the surroundings.

Ryan checked his watch. "We left two-and-a-half hours ago. How long do you think we stopped for you to take photos and at the viewpoint?"

Shandra thought about it and said, "I'd say altogether, maybe half an hour?"

"Then if we ride straight to this spot tomorrow, we should reach it in two hours."

"Sounds good to me."

Shandra didn't pay as much attention to her surroundings the rest of the trip. She was too busy remembering the site and running through the dream she'd had the night before.

The hunting lodge appeared in front of them as the sun began to cast shadows around the building and the trees. Movement in the shadow of the barn caught her attention. Before she could focus on the shape, Hawke's dog trotted out of the shadow to greet them.

Rusk rode his horse over to the far side of the corral, away from the dog.

Shandra wondered if he was frightened of dogs or had another reason for staying away from the canine.

Ryan dismounted and captured the reins of her horse.

She swung her feet to the ground and patted the dog's wide head. "You're making me miss my dog even more," she said.

Hawke walked out of the barn, his saddlebag slung over his shoulder. "Clive, I'm bunking with you tonight," he said.

Shandra nudged Ryan. "Do you think we should tell him that I might have found the cache from my dream?" she whispered.

Ryan shook his head. "No sense saying anything until we know something for sure."

"Where did you disappear to today?" Shandra asked Hawke.

Chapter Ten

Hawke stopped not far from Shandra, but he studied the hiker, trying to make himself as small as possible at the end of the corral. The footprints he'd followed before lunch had brought him in a circle back to the lodge. The so-called hiker was one of his suspects. From the tread on his hiking boots, which Hawke had checked out while the man was horseback riding, the hiker had been the person who met Doolie, followed him, and then made the circle.

He shifted his attention to Shandra. "I've been following the tracks. They never lie." He shot a glance at the hiker and smiled at the woman before heading to the bunkhouse.

Footsteps outside the door and the door opening, revealed the person he'd figured would follow him.

"Detective Greer, I imagine you would like to know more than what I told your wife." Hawke hung his hat on the bunk post and motioned to a small table with four chairs in the corner near the wood stove.

Greer took a seat. "Should we be keeping an eye on Rusk?"

"That the hiker?" Hawke had yet to be introduced to the man.

"Yes. He was asking some interesting questions and said he knew Charlie. Met him at the Blue Elk." Greer had a look on his face that said he didn't believe the hiker.

"I can't say Charlie never went to the Blue Elk Tavern for sure, but I can guarantee you that Doolie spent a good deal of time there in the off season." Yes, from the tracks, he had a notion Doolie had struck up some kind of deal with the hiker.

Hawke studied the detective. He had something else bothering him. "What else?"

The man's head jerked up from where he'd been running a finger up and down a crack in the table. Greer returned his scrutiny.

"There's something you want to tell me," Hawke offered.

"Yes and no." Ryan was torn. Hawke had passed off Shandra's dream when Ryan had brought it up earlier. Which was why he'd planned to wait to say anything until they'd discovered if there really was a cache behind the boulder. While he believed in her dreams because he'd witnessed how they had helped reveal clues to many of the murders they'd both been involved in, it didn't mean Hawke, even with his heritage, would also believe.

"Yes, you know something you should tell me?" Hawke prodded.

"I don't have anything concrete. But tomorrow I

might." He would have laid into a suspect or another police officer if they'd said this to him.

Hawke leaned back, studying him. "Nothing concrete. Where did your information come from? Not something you yourself have seen."

Ryan glanced down at the newly placed ring on his finger. He'd never told anyone he worked with or for about Shandra's dreams.

"What has your wife told you? Is this about the dream you were telling me about before?" Hawke asked quietly.

He released the ring he'd been moving back and forth on his finger and sighed. "I've never told anyone about her dreams before, but perhaps you can understand better than any of my colleagues back in Idaho."

Hawke nodded, "Go on."

"Shandra's grandmother comes to her in dreams. But only when we seem to be caught up in a murder investigation—"

"You say we. Is she also a police officer?"

"No. The first time we met, a local Barney Fife had her cuffed and was ready to haul her off for a gallery owner's death. But the evidence at the scene clearly proved she hadn't killed the woman. Her grandmother came to her then with clues that helped to solve the murder. And there have been others since."

"And what did she see here? About this one?" Hawke asked.

"She rode up to an area on a mule—"

"Clive said that Doolie had taken a mule," Hawke interrupted.

"Yes. She said she rode up on a mule to a boulder,

and behind the boulder there were items cached. Like he, Doolie, had been stealing things from the lodge and hiding them to sell." Ryan studied the State Trooper. He appeared to be taking it all in. There wasn't any skepticism on his face. "One of the items she said looked like a box with bags of gold."

Hawke's attention shot to him. "How did she know about the gold?"

Ryan stared at the trooper. "What gold?"

"I bet Ms. Singer didn't even know it existed. Come on." Hawke stood and strode to the bunkhouse door. "The only people he told about it were me and Doolie. I don't even think Clive knew about it."

Ryan followed the man's long strides across the space between the bunkhouse and the lodge.

They entered the lodge and Hawke didn't stop until he stood beside the ladder Dani stood atop. "Ms. Singer would you come down?" He nodded to Ryan. "Find your wife. I want a list of what she saw."

Ryan nodded and entered the room they were staying in. Shandra sat at the small desk, staring out the window. "Hawke wants a list of the items you saw in your dream."

She spun around. "You told him?"

"He could tell I was holding something back and when I mentioned the gold, he about sprung out of his skin. It appears only Charlie, Doolie, and Hawke knew about the gold. Which made him believe, or will make him believe, your dream when it isn't where Charlie kept it."

Shandra jotted down the items she remembered from the dream and stood, holding the list in her hand. "Let's go."

Hawke and Dani stood hands on hips, glaring at one another.

"What's wrong?" Shandra asked, walking over and standing beside the two.

"Ms. Singer won't give me permission to look in her room." Hawke's glare didn't leave her cousin's face.

"Dani, this is important. Not only for finding Doolie's killer, but to help the lodge," Shandra said, hoping her cousin would give in. For some reason the Fish and Wildlife State Trooper and her cousin had gotten off to a bad start.

"He has to apologize for blaming me for his not being notified about Charlie's death. I had nothing to do with it." Dani stood, feet apart, hands on hips, no doubt a stance she'd taken more than once as a female officer.

Shandra's gaze bounced back and forth between them. She threw her hands in the air, then handed the list to Hawke. "Here is the list." She grasped Dani's arm and said, "Come on. Lead the way to your room."

Dani humphed, but walked out of the great room and down the hall.

Hawke and Ryan followed them.

"What are you looking for?" Dani asked.

Once they were all in the room, even though it was small and crowded, Hawke closed the door and spoke in a low voice. "Charlie had a box with small bags of gold hidden in this room. We have reason to believe Doolie stole it."

Dani's eyes widened, and she started to shake her head. "He could have come in here any time I was off picking up supplies or guests." Her eyes narrowed. "Do you think Leslie knew about it?"

"As far as I know, only Charlie, Doolie, and I knew of its existence. It was passed down to Charlie from his grandfather who had this lodge before him." Hawke eased by everyone in the three feet between the bed and the wall. "It should be under the floorboard, under the bed, in the far corner."

They all moved to the end of the bed as he pulled and then pushed it to the other side. He crouched in the corner and using a knife from the sheath in his boot, he pried up the floorboard. "It's gone."

"Why that little thieving bastard," Dani said, adding a few more expletives.

Hawke grinned and pointed a finger at her. "Good girls don't talk that way."

Dani stared at him. "You sound like Grandmother Singer."

He laughed.

Shandra laughed, too. "It sounds like all of our grandmothers."

"Take a look at the list Shandra gave Hawke. Any idea if those items are missing?" Ryan said, always one to stay focused on business.

Hawke handed the paper to Dani.

She shook her head. "I don't remember seeing either of these. But he could have stolen them before I took over the lodge."

Ryan glanced at Hawke. "We were planning to ride out and check the boulder tomorrow."

"I'll go with you," Hawke said.

"What boulder? What are you talking about?" Dani asked.

Shandra shared a glance with Ryan. Did she dare tell her distant cousin, something she told few people?

He shook his head.

"We have an idea about where these items might be," was all Shandra shared.

Dani stared at each one in turn. "That's all you'll tell me?"

"That's all we know," Hawke said. "Not a word of any of this to anyone. Not even Clive and Leslie."

"Mr. Rusk has been asking all kinds of questions since you returned from the ride," Dani said.

"What kind of questions?" Hawke asked.

"How I came to inherit the lodge? Why I didn't let Clive and Doolie take over?" She shook her head. "They just seemed odd coming from a stranger."

"I think he and Doolie were friends," Hawke offered.

Shandra faced him. "How?"

He shook his head. "You might be able to learn everything about a case from your husband, but you won't from me."

Heat infused her cheeks. She'd never had anyone call her on that before.

Ryan opened the door. "I suggest we try and get information out of Rusk at dinner."

"That's what I was thinking," Hawke said, shoving the bed back in place.

Chapter Eleven

Dinner wasn't as eventful as Shandra had hoped. Rusk ducked all the personal questions they tossed at him and left as soon as he'd eaten his meal.

Clive leaned over the table, poking the tabletop with a finger as soon as the man's back had disappeared out the door and the front door creaked open and shut. "He would have never visited with Charlie at the Blue Elk in Winslow. Charlie and the owner had been on bad terms for years. He's a liar."

Shandra smiled at the old wrangler. That's why he'd had the funny expression on his face earlier today when the hiker had mentioned it.

"And he was in the barn when we returned from the ride, going through it like he was a termite inspector." Clive picked up his cup of coffee. "I don't trust him."

Leslie walked into the dining room from the kitchen.

"That was a fine meal," Clive said to her.

She nodded and in her grumpy, uncivil way picked up the dishes and walked back through the kitchen door.

Shandra studied her cousin who had been quiet all through the meal. "Why do you keep Leslie? She isn't very hospitable."

"Doolie asked me to keep her on. I didn't realize they were married until now." Dani stared at the kitchen door. "He's gone and I think it's time for her to go, too."

"Don't send her away until I've finished my investigation," Hawke said.

"Is she a suspect?" Dani asked.

"Everyone on this mountain is a suspect," Hawke replied. His gaze leveled on Dani, then on everyone still at the table.

Clive laughed. "You ain't serious. This here is a cop from Idaho and I didn't have a big enough beef with Doolie to kill him."

"I noticed you didn't mention Ms. Singer. Do you have reason to believe she killed Doolie?" Hawke asked.

Shandra sucked in air. Did the trooper actually think Dani had killed the man?

"I figured she was a given to not kill him. Shoot, it would have been Doolie killing her that made sense. He wanted the lodge. He was on a drunk for a week after the will was read." Clive nodded.

"No one is a given, Clive." Hawke stood. "I'll be in the bunkhouse if anyone needs me." He left the room.

Shandra felt Dani relax. "He doesn't believe you are a suspect," she said, trying to help ease the woman's mind.

"He doesn't like me," Dani said.

"A good cop doesn't let that interfere with an investigation. He seems to be a good, thorough cop." Ryan stood. "I'm going for a walk. You want to join me?" he asked Shandra.

"I'd love to." She stood and put a hand on Dani's shoulder. "Don't worry. We'll get this figured out."

"I hope so." Dani stood. "I think I'll go for a walk, too. I need to clear my head."

Clive stood. "Guess I'll call it a day. See you all in the morning."

They parted ways at the porch. Clive headed to the bunkhouse. Dani headed to the trail that circled behind the lodge.

Ryan grasped Shandra's hand and led her to the spot where he'd witnessed Rusk coming from the day before.

"You're sure we won't get lost?" Shandra asked.

He squeezed her hand. "I was a boy scout. I can't get lost in the woods."

"It's going to be dark soon."

"We're not going that far." He studied the ground, but he didn't see anything. How the hell had Hawke followed a trail to here?

Instead of following a trail that he couldn't see, Ryan moved along the inside of the woods to the back of the bunkhouse.

"What are we doing back here?" Shandra asked.

"I don't know. Something feels off with this whole thing. How did Doolie get from the motel the night before to here so fast? We flew in. He didn't. It took the retrieval team half a day to get here. That would mean, he couldn't have been here until at the earliest noon. I'd sure like to know what the coroner had to say about time of death." Ryan didn't have any means of finding that out, but he wondered if Hawke did.

"Time of death was between eleven and two," Hawke's voice said from the corner of the building.

Ryan turned slowly toward him. "How did Doolie get up here so fast?"

Hawke walked toward them. "He knew this mountain like a farmer knows his land. I'm sure with the mule he stole, he came up the canyon and mountain on a trail only he and a few hunters know."

"Do you think Rusk killed him?" Ryan asked.

"Where's that mule?" Shandra asked.

Hawke responded to Shandra first. "The mule is in the corral." He shifted his attention to Ryan. "Don't know if Rusk is the murderer. I've been following his tracks the last two days but as skittish as he was when we asked him questions, I can't see him sticking around after killing someone."

"That's what I was thinking. He doesn't act like a killer, but he does act like he's up to something." Ryan studied the man in the growing dusk. "Do you have a way to run a check on him?"

"I radioed what little we know to dispatch and asked for someone to do a background check on him." Hawke raised one wide hand. "It's up to us to figure this out the old-fashioned way. Watch people, ask questions, and follow leads. My gut tells me the answers are on the mountain, not in the valley."

He'd had similar feelings. Which if they ruled out Rusk and Dani, that only left two other suspects.

~*~

The following morning, Shandra was up as soon as

the sun peeked through the bedroom window. She hadn't had any dreams with Ella in them during the night and took that to mean, their checking out the boulder was the correct action to take.

Ryan rolled out of bed right behind her. "The sooner we get up to that spot and check it out, the quicker we'll know how to proceed."

There wasn't any coffee set out. Shandra opened the kitchen door expecting to find Leslie making breakfast but the room was empty. She went about finding the coffee and tea bags but discovered the wood cook stove wasn't stoked enough to boil the water. She found a package of store-bought Danish and carried that out to the dining room.

Ryan entered the room. "Hawke has the horses saddled and ready."

"Leslie wasn't in the kitchen and hasn't started the cookstove. Looks like all we get are these." She held the package out.

"Hawke had a cup of coffee." Ryan left the room.

Shandra followed him all the way out to the barn. She held out the pastries. "This is all I could find. Where did you get coffee?"

"Clive has a pot on the stove in the bunkhouse." Hawke took one of the pastries while Ryan strode toward the bunkhouse.

"Aren't you going to get coffee?" Hawke asked before taking a bite.

"I'm not a coffee drinker. Food fuels me." She pulled out a danish and had it half eaten by the time Ryan returned with an enamelware cup.

He grabbed a pastry and ate it along with swallowing down the coffee.

"I didn't find Leslie in the kitchen," Shandra said to Hawke. "What time does she usually get up and start cooking?"

"Now. What about Ms. Singer? Was she moving about yet?"

She didn't like that Hawke still thought of Dani as one of the suspects.

"I didn't see either one of them," Shandra replied.

"We might want to make sure they are okay before we head out." Hawke threw the last of his coffee on the ground and handed his cup to Ryan. "Take this back to the bunkhouse. Shandra and I will check on the women."

Ryan hesitated, but did as he was asked.

Hawke put a hand on her arm. "Check their bedrooms, I'll wait in the great room."

"What do you want me to say for looking in on them in their rooms?"

"That I wanted to make sure they were okay before we went on a ride. The truth is always your best answer."

She smiled. That sounded like something her grandmother or Aunt Jo would say. She went down the hall to Dani's room and knocked. There wasn't an answer. She opened the door. The room was neat and tidy. Either she'd gotten up and already made the bed or she never went to sleep last night. Worried, she walked out the back door and knocked on the outhouses. Nothing. She heard water running and realized someone was in the shower. A rap on the door and the water stopped.

"Who's there?" Dani called out.

"Just Shandra. I was wondering where you were."

"Is there a problem?" Worry coated her words.

"No. Hawke, Ryan, and I are going for a horseback ride. We'll see you about noon."

Dani's wet head appeared out the door. "Don't you want breakfast before you leave?"

"We tried to get some, but we can't find Leslie." Shandra studied her cousin. She appeared as perplexed as the rest of them.

"She wasn't in the kitchen? Did you try her room to see if she isn't feeling well?"

"That was my next stop." Shandra started to back away.

"Just a minute. I'll come with you." Dani's head disappeared and within two minutes she appeared dressed in jeans, a long-sleeved t-shirt, and her slippers.

They returned to the lodge and found Hawke pacing in the great room. They ignored him to continue into the dining room and kitchen.

"Her room is right here off the kitchen." Dani opened the door. The room was empty. "Where could she be?"

Hawke wedged himself in the small door frame. "No cook?"

Shandra spun around. "No. Do you think she's in danger?"

"Won't know until we go look for her." He backed out of the door and into the kitchen.

Shandra and Dani followed.

"What about Rusk? Is he here?" Shandra asked.

"One way to find out." Hawke strode through the dining room to the great room and pounded on guest room number two.

"What?" Rusk's half-asleep voice called out.

"Are you alone in there?" Hawke asked and tried the door knob. It was locked.

"What the hell?" Rusk flung the door open. "Who the hell do you think I'd have in my room?"

"The cook is missing," Hawke said.

Rusk cringed. "I'm not that desperate."

"When was the last time you saw her?" Shandra asked, hoping the man could shed some light on the disappearance.

The hiker narrowed his eyes. "What is this? You couldn't learn anything from me last night at dinner so you try and pin a missing old lady on me? Screw you!" He slammed the door and the sound of the lock clicking in place said he wasn't interested in any more company.

"I'll see if I can find any sign of where she went." Hawke strode across the great room and out the front of the lodge.

Shandra turned to Dani. "I guess we need to make breakfast." She was upset that they couldn't go to the boulder, but finding the woman, considering her husband had been found dead not three days ago, was the top priority right now.

Chapter Twelve

Ryan left the horses Hawke had saddled tied to the corral and decided to follow the path that led from the corral around the back of the house. He didn't know if the woman was someone who took a walk to start her day, but if she had, a wild animal could have attacked.

Out of the corner of his eye, he caught a glimpse of Hawke scanning the ground. Would they both end up in the same place?

Ryan strode into the forest on the trail. He scanned the ground to see if there were any new tracks going the same direction as him. There were many traces of wild animals using and crossing the path, but he didn't see any shoe prints pointed down the path.

He came out at the area where he and Shandra had started the trail the first day they arrived. Everyone was in front of the lodge talking. Hurrying over, he caught the tail end of Clive's comment.

"...that young gelding we've been having

problems with is gone."

"What do you mean gone?" Dani asked.

"It ain't in the corral. And the smaller saddle, that we use for the kids, it's gone, too."

"Looks like Leslie decided to go for a horseback ride early this morning or last night." Hawke strode toward the horses tied to the corral. "My guess is she wanted to get to that boulder before we did."

Ryan nodded and headed to the gelding he'd ridden the day before. Shandra was right behind him, swinging up on the mare she'd used. Hawke swung up on the big sturdy gelding he'd arrived on.

Hawke patted his saddlebag. "If she or the horse comes back, radio me. Clive knows the frequency."

Hawke motioned for Ryan to take the lead.

He started his gelding out at a trot. He heard the others fall into the cadence behind him. Lucky for him, the trail was well defined.

As they neared the high point where they'd stopped to check the view, Ryan spotted a horse with a saddle, grazing.

He stopped and waited for the other two to ride up beside him. "Any idea if that's the horse that's missing?"

Hawke nodded. "I saw him in the corral yesterday." He slipped off his horse, told the dog to stay, and slowly walked toward the animal. The wind carried sounds back to them.

"What is he saying?" Ryan asked Shandra.

"It sounds like what Andy and Uncle Martin say to horses when they are calming them down. It's in the old language." Shandra was becoming more and more impressed with this State Trooper. It seemed he carried a lot of his heritage with him.

Hawke patted the horse on the neck before taking the reins in his hand and leading the animal back to them. "Hold him while I look over the edge."

The unemotional way he said the statement, sent a chill up Shandra's spine. He'd steeled himself for the worst. Leslie being thrown over the cliff.

Shandra stayed by her horse, staring at the man as he approached the edge and gazed down.

Ryan stepped up beside her, wrapping an arm around her shoulders.

Hawke lowered to his knees and then his belly as he eased his upper body out over the edge.

Shandra put her arm around Ryan's waist, willing the man to not find Leslie's crumpled body.

Hawke returned to his knees and stood. "We'll need a rope. I think she's still alive. Looked like her hand moved."

Ryan released her. "I can go down to her. I know how to rock climb."

The trooper walked over to his saddlebag and pulled out a roll of parachute cord, carabiner, and a harness. "The rocks are going to move under your feet. Better go down to the right of her. It's closer to a tree to tie off on."

Shandra watched the two men work together to tie one end of the rope to the tree and get Ryan into the climbing harness.

"It looks like you're going to be a bit short of where she's laying," Hawke said.

"Luckily, she's a small woman." Ryan attached the carabiner to the harness and tied the cord through the metal fastener.

Shandra removed the sweatshirt tied around her waist. "Here, you could use this as a sling to bring her back up."

Ryan kissed her, took the shirt, and looped the arms through his belt. He moved to step over the edge.

"Wait a minute." Hawke walked over and handed him a pair of gloves.

"Thanks." Ryan shoved his hands into the gloves, secured the paracord in his hands, and disappeared over the edge.

Shandra's heart raced with fear and worry. She didn't know whether to stay with the horses, watch from the edge, or just remain out of the way and pray. It would have been useless to try and talk Ryan out of being the one to go down the cliff after the woman. He was younger and lighter than Hawke. It made sense he was the one to go. Knowing that didn't make her any less nervous.

~*~

Ryan took his time finding footholds. He didn't want a rock rolling down and causing more injury to the woman. They had a lot of questions for her.

He glanced up. Hawke and Shandra were both on their bellies watching his descent. He was about to the end of the rope when he spotted the cook sprawled on a small flat spot to his left. Before releasing the rope, he made a mental path to where the woman lay. It was mostly dirt and loose rocks, but one slip, and he could end up twenty feet farther down or at the bottom.

"You can do it," Shandra said from up above.

He gave her a thumb's up and released the rope, slowly maneuvering across the side of the cliff to the unconscious woman.

89

The first thing he did was check her body for breaks. It appeared her left arm and leg could be broken. He would have rather been able to call in a life flight helicopter but knew her chances were better if they got her back to the lodge and Dani flew her out.

He eased Shandra's sweatshirt under the woman's back below her arm pits. Then leaned down and tied the sweatshirt arms around his neck. The woman cried out when he stood up, but he had to carry her this way to get her to the top of the cliff.

A glance at the top revealed Hawke and Shandra were no longer watching. He'd hoped for a little help getting up the hill with the added weight. It was slow progress over to the rope. Their combined weight slid them down the hill twice, making him have to work even harder to get to the rope.

Once there he hooked into the carabiner and began the ascent. The cording became taut. He wrapped a half-hitch at the carabiner to keep the rope from slipping out of his fingers. The tension grew tighter. He felt a tug pulling him up as he moved his legs to gain purchase on the side of the cliff. The lifting helped him half walk up the side.

The top came into view. He willed his legs to not give out and pushed one more step. His head cleared the top and Hawke ran over. He grabbed the sweatshirt over Ryan's neck, pulling Leslie over the edge, and then Ryan.

The woman moaned.

Ryan scanned the area and saw the reason he'd come up the cliff so easily. Hawke had tied the rope to his horse. Shandra was under a tree tying branches together.

"I think her left arm and leg are broken. Must have hit her head too, from the bruise and her unconscious state." Ryan stood, untying the rope, and slipping out of the harness.

"Shandra is making a travois. We'll take Leslie back to the lodge and have Dani fly her out. Then we'll head back out to finish what we started." Hawke walked over to Shandra. "Is that ready?"

"I think so. I've never built a travois before." Shandra stood, her brow wrinkled in a frown, but her eyes were lit with excitement.

She hurried over to him and gave him a hug. "Good job, detective," she teased.

"Thanks." He kissed the top of her head.

Hawke led his horse over to the contraption Shandra had built. "Jack has had to pull a few of these." He used leather lacing from his saddlebag to tie the ends of the travois to the stirrups. When the Native American gurney was ready, he led his horse over next to Leslie.

They lifted her onto the woven limbs. Shandra tucked her sweatshirt around the woman's upper body.

Everyone mounted up. Ryan took the front, leading Leslie's horse. Shandra fell in behind the rider-less horse, and Hawke pulled the travois at the rear of the procession.

Ryan kept the pace at a slow walk to not jar the woman any more than was necessary. He wondered when she'd left on the horse. Last night or this morning? If this morning, she wouldn't have been laying exposed to the weather as long. If last night…there could be more complications than broken bones and a concussion. But why had she gone out at all?

Walking out of the trees at the lodge, he'd expected to be met by Clive at least. No one greeted them.

Hawke dismounted in front of the helicopter. He seemed just as puzzled. "Shandra go get Dani. Tell her she has to fly Leslie to a hospital. Ryan find Clive."

Shandra took off to the house and Ryan headed to the barn.

Chapter Thirteen

Shandra ran into the lodge.

"Dani! Dani!" she called, seeing the woman wasn't up on the ladder in the great room. She slammed the doors open on her cousin's office and bedroom.

Nothing.

She banged out the back door, looking in the outhouses and shower.

Nothing.

Had she and Clive gone out looking for Leslie?

She bolted back through the house, stopping at the other guest room.

She knocked.

No one said, "Come in."

With a twist of the knob, she flung the door open.

The bed was unmade.

But what caught her attention was the lack of anything in the room. No shoes, no backpack, nothing that showed someone was using the space.

Breathless from all the hurrying, she jogged out to Hawke. "There is no one in there. All of Rusk's things are gone."

Ryan joined them. "I can't find Clive anywhere."

Hawke cursed and said, "Let's put Leslie in her bed. Either of you much good at first aid?"

Shandra knew Ryan was more skilled at it than she was, but he'd need to help Hawke search for Dani and Clive. "I'll see what I can do."

Hawke stopped reaching for the woman and straightened, looking her in the eye. "You ever set a broken bone?"

She gulped. "No."

He turned his narrowed gaze on Ryan. "You?"

"Once."

Hawke cursed again. He stared at Ryan. "Do you know how to work a radio?"

"Yes."

"Then while we get her in bed and set her breaks, you go call anyone you can get a hold of on the radio. Tell them we need to evac a woman with multiple injuries, and we need a search and rescue team in here to look for two people taken hostage."

Shandra stared at Hawke. "Hostage?"

"Do you have a better idea of what happened?" He scowled at her.

"No."

"Come on, let's get her in the house." Hawke reached under the older woman gently, lifting her in his arms like a small child.

Shandra ran ahead, opening the doors for him.

Ryan headed down the hall to the office.

Since Hawke said they would deal with Leslie's

injuries, Shandra figured he needed her help.

The state trooper was gentle settling the woman on the narrow bed. He took off his hat, placed it on the small chest of drawers, and rolled up the sleeves of his lightweight denim shirt.

"See if you can find any kind of a first aid kit around here. And pain pills. I'm going to go look for limbs or sticks we can use to splint the arm and leg." He strode out of the room.

Shandra checked all the cupboards in the kitchen. She didn't find anything. Her next guess was the office and then Dani's room.

Ryan was rummaging through the office desk.

"What's wrong," Shandra asked.

"The microphone is missing and it doesn't come on when I flick the switch. The radio has been sabotaged." Ryan opened another drawer. "If the radio worked I could morse code with some wire. I'm looking for wire and hoping I can get the thing working."

Shandra found the first aid kit.

Ryan was still rummaging in the desk drawers when she left the room.

She moved on to Dani's room and found a bottle of ibuprofen. She had a feeling Hawke had hoped for something stronger, but Dani was a healthy person.

Returning to the cook's bedroom, she found Hawke measuring two sticks about an inch in diameter to the woman's lower arm. He used the knife from his boot to chop them shorter before he picked up two pieces of wood which appeared to be kindling to start a fire.

"If there's gauze in that kit, wrap it around these two sticks to make them comfortable against her leg. If there's no gauze, find towels to wrap around and tape to them."

She nodded and dug in the bag. There was only a little gauze. Not even enough to cover one stick. She had a thought. "Are there any vet supplies in the barn?"

"Yes. In the tack room there's a box." Hawke looked up from chopping the stick. "Good idea."

"I come up with one every now and then." She jogged out of the lodge and over to the barn. The tack room was easy to find. She looked around and found an old wooden box with a leather hinged lid. Inside were rolls of vet wrap, self-adhering bandaging used on animals. She also found Bute, a horse pain killer. She grabbed all the rolls of vet wrap and the Bute.

Hawke had retrieved a pan of water and a rag. He was wiping the blood away from the cracked, bruised skin on Leslie's head. "Find anything?"

"Vet wrap for the sticks. Can a person use Bute?"

"Good on the wrap. No, on the Bute. I'll start the cookstove while you wrap the sticks. Do all four. If we can make tea, we can crush the ibuprofen into it and drizzle it down her throat." Hawke left the room.

Shandra went to work wrapping the sticks as he'd asked.

A hand grabbed her arm.

She stared into the pain dulled eyes of Leslie.

"Did you find it?" she whispered.

"What?"

"My gold. It was Doolie's. Now it's mine." The woman's face pinched in pain and her eyes closed.

"Leslie!" Shandra felt the arm dangling over the bed for a pulse. There was still a weak one.

"What are you calling her for?" Hawke asked,

96

entering the room.

"She woke up and asked if I'd found the gold. She said it was hers because Doolie was dead." Shandra held up the wrapped sticks. "It never belonged to Doolie. He stole it. She must have known."

Hawke stared down at the woman. "This is the hard part of my job. Helping people who might have committed a crime." He put a hand on the wall and one knee on the far side of the bed. "You'll have to hold her shoulders down when I do the initial pull to set the bone. Then I'll need you to hand me what I ask for."

Shandra nodded and put her hands on the woman's shoulders. She didn't watch, only felt when the woman tried to raise up.

"Okay, hand me the two smaller sticks, then the tape."

She glanced at Hawke as she handed the sticks to him. Sweat beaded his brow.

They had her arm secured when Ryan entered the room. "The radio has been disabled. I can't find supplies to get it running."

Hawke cursed and shook his head. "After we get this leg set, I'll see if I can find their trail."

"What are we going to do?" Shandra asked.

"You'll stay here and tend Leslie." Hawke moved to stand at the end of the bed. "First, this leg has to be set. Same as before."

Shandra put her hands on the woman's shoulders.

Ryan stepped up to the bed to hold Leslie's upper leg while Hawke set the lower.

The woman cried out but didn't wake up again. Shandra wondered if she'd daydreamed the woman grabbing her arm and talking to her. How greedy must the woman be to worry about the gold and not her health?

Hawke stepped away from the bed. Leslie had rainbow colored vet wrapped sticks taped to her arm and leg. "Cover her up, make some tea. Crumble two pills up and put them in the drink. Get as much down her as you can. Do that every three hours. If she comes around, try to get her to eat something." Hawk rolled his sleeves down and grabbed his hat. "I'll get my radio out of my pack. Not sure if we'll be able to contact help with it, but I'll leave it with you. When I find the tracks, I'll come let you know which way I'm headed."

"I'll come with you. We have no idea if Rusk is working alone or with someone," Ryan said.

Shandra's heart lurched. She didn't really want to stay here by herself. "What if Rusk comes back here?"

Ryan studied Shandra. He was torn. He wanted to help his fellow law enforcement officer, but at the same time, he didn't want to leave his new wife alone either.

"I'll stay. Pack food for Hawke."

~*~

Hawke didn't wait around for the newlyweds to work things out. Charlie's niece could be in trouble and he owed the dead old coot. The man had taken him in during a freak snow storm that had caught him off guard and kept him at the lodge for a week before it was safe enough to travel back down.

If Rusk had Ms. Singer and Clive, would he go back the way he'd come? But how had he gotten here? He said from Minam. Hawke had asked Sullen to run all the license plates on the vehicles parked at the beginning of the trailhead. Last night when Hawke called to find out what they knew so far, Sullen had said none of the plates were registered to a Harris Rusk. And he was waiting for any hits on the name.

Hawke marched over to his pack by the bed he'd slept in. The zipper was open. He cursed, already knowing what he would find.

His radio was gone.

It looked like taking care of Leslie and finding the others was up to him and the two in the lodge. He knew there was no way he could send either one of them out of here on a horse to get help. If they had come in by horseback, he knew the woman would be able to find her way back out, but they flew in. He doubted they would know which trails to follow and get help here any faster than if he tracked them.

He went back to the front of the lodge and studied the tracks. There was Rusk's boot print. He'd followed it enough to recognize it. There was a cowboy boot print. Rusk's print stepped partially in it. That would be Clive's. From the heaviness of the weight on the outside edges, Clive was working to maintain his balance. Rusk must have knocked him out. Next to the cowboy boot print was an athletic shoe print. That would be Ms. Singer.

He followed the trio into the edge of the tree line and determined which direction they were headed. Southeast.

Hawke returned to the lodge. Ryan had a pack on his back and Shandra stood by the fireplace.

"I'm going with you. Shandra can take care of Leslie until we get back." Ryan glanced at his wife and smiled.

From the look on Shandra's face, Hawke thought the man was making a big mistake. He'd lost his wife over his dedication to his job. "You're sure? You could stay here and see if you can get the radio working. They took mine."

Ryan stepped forward. "All the more reason I need to go with you. Rusk must have someone he plans to contact."

Hawke wasn't going to argue. They were wasting time. "Keep the woodstove going. Do you know how to shoot?" he asked Shandra.

"I can shoot. Stoking the stove with wood I've done before."

Her confidant words didn't reflect in her face.

He nodded. "Then we'll see you when we've found them."

Ryan strode across the room and kissed his wife.

She ran a hand down his arm. "I'll be fine. Just be careful."

"I will." The detective spun and followed Hawke out of the lodge.

"You sure this is what you want to do?" he asked, not wanting to cause the break up in their marriage.

"She told me to go. I wanted to stay with her." He laughed half-heartedly. "I'm being a good husband and doing what she says."

"They don't always say what they really want." Didn't he know that. But when his wife said she wanted out of the marriage, she'd meant that.

"She's scared for me, not her." Ryan had to believe that. And that she was just as safe here as if he were beside her. She knew he'd go crazy knowing Hawke was out here alone doing a job Ryan had been trained to do.

"That's how I lost my wife. She couldn't take the

fact I was always in danger and put my job before her." Hawke walked to the corral where the horses were still tied and whistled to his dog.

"How long ago was that?" Ryan had wondered if the man had a wife.

"Twenty-five years ago." Hawke swung up on his horse.

Ryan mounted his and asked. "You never remarried?"

"Didn't want to make the same mistake." Hawke set out in a southeasterly direction.

Watching the man lean down and peer at the ground, Ryan tried doing the same but he saw very little. What was he looking at? Whatever it was they were now veering to the left.

"Do you have any idea where they are going?" he asked.

"If they hadn't turned, they might have been going to a bald peak where someone could pick them up with a helicopter." Hawke pointed to the ground. "He's pushing them hard and something's wrong with Clive. His feet are dragging."

"Do you think he was shot?" Ryan asked.

"No. There'd be blood."

He sat back in the saddle and followed the State Trooper. The man seemed to know what was happening by staring at the tracks.

Chapter Fourteen

Shandra made the tea and held the woman up with an arm behind her back, dribbling the tea and pain killer into Leslie's mouth. The liquid trickled out the corners of the injured woman's mouth, but she felt confident that some had gone into the cook's system.

After making Leslie comfortable, Shandra went into Dani's office and dug around looking for the manual to the radio. As orderly as her cousin was and the fact the radio looked new, Dani would have the manual within easy reach.

And she did.

Shandra opened it up, and page by page, checked each knob, cord, and transistor on the transmitter. She discovered the missing part besides the microphone. Knowing her cousin came from a life of government bureaucracy and living in a place with limited access to parts, there had to be a box of transistors here somewhere. And maybe even another microphone.

Ryan hadn't found anything searching through the drawers in the desk. She started methodically going through the closets in the house. She came up without anything that looked remotely like the parts in the manual. Maybe she kept things like that in the barn.

Checking on Leslie and seeing she still remained unconscious, Shandra headed to the barn. When she'd gone to the tack room before, looking for the vet supplies, she hadn't looked around. Now she searched the room. All the shelves and boxes.

Nothing.

It didn't make sense. Dani would have spare parts. Where did she keep supplies for the helicopter and plane? She hadn't found anything that looked like aircraft parts.

She walked around the outside of the barn and found a door on the side next to where the helicopter sat. A yank on the big wood door revealed the workshop for the aircraft. It had barrels of fuel and parts. New shelving on one side caught her attention. That's where she found several boxes. One had a microphone and one had transistors.

Back at the office using the manual, she installed the transistor and plugged the microphone in after digging the base of the old microphone cord out of the opening.

Rereading the manual, she figured out how to make a call. Using a list of call numbers taped to the desk beside the radio, she contacted a dispatch.

"Hello. My name is Shandra Higheagle Greer. My husband Ryan Greer and State Trooper Hawke are following a man who took Ms. Dani Singer, owner of Charlie's Hunting Lodge, and her wrangler, Clive, hostage. We don't know if he will hurt them or what the hiker, Harris Rusk, plans to do. We found the cook, Leslie, with a broken arm and leg and would like Life Flight to fly to the lodge and pick her up."

The radio crackled and a man's voice came through. "We'll send Life Flight as soon as we can. Did Hawke request Search and Rescue?"

"He did. But when he left the radio wasn't working." She glanced at the clock on the desk. "They left nearly three hours ago. It's getting late, will a helicopter be able to land now?"

"I'll let you know on both counts."

"Thank you."

She'd been working on the radio for three hours. She needed to check on Leslie and give her more tea with pain killer.

Walking into the cook's bedroom, she found the woman's eyes open.

"How did I get here?" she asked.

"Hawke, Ryan, and I found you. Ryan carried you up the side of the cliff." Shandra set the cup of tea down on the table next to the bed. "Do you think you could drink tea and broth if I prop you up?"

The woman nodded, but winced, as Shandra slipped an arm behind her back and helped her sit up enough to drink. When the tea was gone, she lowered the woman.

"I'll find something for you to eat. All that pain medicine on an empty stomach can't be good." Shandra stood.

The woman reached out with her good arm. "Where is everyone?"

Shandra wasn't sure how much to say. "We believe

the hiker Rusk has Dani and Clive."

The woman's eyes widened. "He's going after the gold."

This was a good time to pretend she didn't know anything. "What gold?"

The woman stared at her, but her eyelids started to droop. "Doesn't matter."

Shandra wanted to shake the woman back to consciousness but knew that wouldn't be good for her already jarred head.

What she wanted to know was how the woman knew about the gold and did she kill her husband to get her hands on it?

~*~

Ryan was used to riding Huckleberry Mountain with Shandra, but they stopped often. Once Hawke swung up into the saddle of his horse, he'd only stepped down once and that was to check the prints closer. He'd only been off long enough for Ryan to start to swing his leg over to dismount and the man was back on his horse and moving again.

"Is there a chance we can stretch our legs a minute?" Ryan asked from behind the State Trooper.

Hawke peered at him over his shoulder and stopped his horse.

Ryan pulled back on the reins and dismounted. His butt was numb and his legs had cramped a mile ago. He walked around raising his legs and massaging his backside.

Hawke dismounted and crouched, looking at the ground. "We're getting closer. The track is fresher. But I don't like that it looks as if Ms. Singer is now helping Clive."

"That could be slowing them down. That's good for us." Ryan continued to work his legs.

Hawke stood. "True." He reached into his saddle bag and handed Ryan a bottle of water and a package of nuts.

"Thanks." He guzzled half the water and ate the nuts, while Hawke sipped his water.

"Are you ready? We're going to lose light soon." Hawke finished off his water and swung up on his horse.

"Yeah." His legs still felt cramped, but they weren't out on a leisurely ride. There could be lives at stake, and he wouldn't be the cause of something happening to one of them.

Back on the horses, Hawke started veering more to the left. Ryan glanced up at the snow peak to the right and recognized it. The trail they followed was circling back toward the hunting lodge. And he'd left Shandra there all alone.

~*~

The growing dusk made it harder for Shandra to see inside the lodge. She'd found a lighter and made the rounds lighting the kerosene lanterns in the cook's bedroom, the kitchen, dining room, and the great room. She wanted things lit up when help came.

She heard the radio crackling as she lit a lantern in the great room. She hurried into the office and lit a lantern there. "This is Shandra, what can you tell me?" she replied.

"Life Flight will be there at first light in the morning. Search and Rescue will also leave the head of the trail at first light. Do you have any coordinates on Hawke?"

That was the worst part. She had no clue where Ryan and Hawke could be. "No. He didn't say which direction they were headed."

"Over. We'll send up a helicopter in the morning to also locate them."

"That would be great. Could you let me know as well?"

"Will do. Talk to you in the morning."

"Thanks."

She leaned back in the chair. "Grandmother watch over Ryan and Hawke tonight." Pushing out of the chair, she went back to lighting the lanterns even though there would be no help coming tonight. Having the place lit up didn't make it feel so lonely.

Back in the kitchen, she warmed up a can of soup and split it between two bowls, putting a slice of homemade bread in the side of each bowl. She put these on a tray she found and carried it into the cook's bedroom.

The woman was awake again.

"I brought you some soup." Shandra set the tray on the bedside table and reached out to help the woman sit up.

"I don't want any soup. I want left alone." Tears had trickled down the side of her head, leaving a wet trail.

"Leslie, you need to be strong. Help will be here in the morning to take you to a medical facility." Shandra put her arm behind the woman's boney back and raised up the pillow to lean her against.

"I don't want anyone to take me anywhere. If I don't have money to live on, then I can't stop working. I'm tired." She closed her eyes and refused the soup when Shandra tried to spoon some into her mouth.

Shandra sat back and stared at the woman. She reminded her of some of the women she'd met on the Colville Reservation. Too stubborn to ask for help and too worn out to want to go on.

She left the soup and tea on the table and took hers on the tray to the great room. Shandra curled her feet underneath her on the couch and sipped the soup, wondering where Ryan was and if they had come upon Dani and the others.

Putting the soup and spoon to the side, she stood. "Just because he took his things doesn't mean he couldn't have left something behind." She retrieved the lighter from the kitchen and walked into the room occupied by Rusk. She lit the lantern on the table by the bed and used it like a flashlight, lighting under the bed, opening the drawers of the chest, and searching each corner.

When that revealed nothing, she took each blanket off the bed, shaking it out, watching to see if anything fell on the floor. The blankets revealed nothing.

However, raising the mattress, she discovered a map.

He'd tucked it away and then in his haste to leave, forgot it.

With the map in one hand and the lantern in the other, she returned to the great room couch. She spread the map across the large wood slab coffee table and placed a lantern at each top corner.

It was a geographical wilderness map of the Wallowa Whitman Forest. Charlie's Hunting Lodge was circled. This had been his destination. Was it to confront or kill Doolie? But why then had he come back?

Blue ink traced his trail to a spot a mile or so from the lodge. It had a small X. Red ink marked a path over the top of the mountain and a red X marked a flat spot on the other side. Could that be where he was headed? If only Hawke had his radio, she could relay what she'd learned.

Shandra's heart raced. Excitement pumped through her veins. Once Leslie was air lifted out of here, she could take a horse and go see if there was gold stashed behind the boulder.

Chapter Fifteen

The morning sun had barely begun to filter through the trees. Ryan stretched, twisted his aching back, and walked behind a tree to relieve himself. It had been years since he'd minimalist camped. He was thankful for the food and water Shandra had packed before they left. And that the nights, while being cool, weren't the same as they would have been a month earlier.

Hawke had already left to inspect the trail on foot. When they'd stopped during the night, he said he thought they weren't that far behind, but didn't want to come upon them in the dark.

Digging in his pack, Ryan pulled out a bag of chocolate chip cookies and bit into one. The sound of trickling water had him wandering to his right. A two feet wide and six-inch deep stream sparkled and wandered through the trees. He knelt and scooped water with his hands. The sting of the cold water caused him to suck in air and pull his hands back. He'd forgotten how cold fresh snow melt could be. Steeling himself for the iciness, he scooped and splashed his face. If he hadn't been awake before, he was now. It felt as if he'd dropped his face in a bowl of ice.

Dog appeared at his side, lapping at the water. The sound of snapping twigs and rustling of forest floor debris brought him to his feet. He glanced over his shoulder.

Hawke led the two horses to the stream. "Your horse needs water, too."

The two animals put their heads down and drank thirstily.

Ryan realized he'd just lost points with the State Trooper for not thinking of his horse. "Sorry, I just followed the sound of the water to see what it was." He took the reins to his horse.

"If you had carried him on your back, I would forgive you, but he carried you." Hawke stared into the trees beyond the stream.

There were times with the State Trooper that Ryan felt like he was at the reservation with Shandra's family. The way they said things held truth and at the same time it shamed him.

"Again, sorry. What did you find out this morning?"

"What I thought last night. I think our friend Rusk is lost. He follows every incline as though his plan was to go to the top of the mountain, but he doesn't know where that is." Hawke smiled. "We are less than a mile behind them. Mount up and we will overtake them soon."

Ryan smiled back. He patted his Glock in his

shoulder holster under his jacket. He'd grabbed the two items out of his duffel bag before they left the lodge.

~*~

Shandra woke, replaying Grandmother's dream. The lodge had been filled with people. Some she'd recognized and some she hadn't. They were looting the place while Dani and Clive were tied to trees watching. She didn't know what it meant other than perhaps someone other than Doolie wanted the lodge and Dani and Clive had no knowledge of them. But who could it be? Since Ryan and Hawke hadn't been in the dream, she had to believe that meant they weren't in trouble, and she would find the gold today.

Dressing, she thought she heard the thump of helicopter blades. She shoved her feet into her boots and ran out the front door. A Life Flight helicopter had landed on Dani's airstrip close to the house. Two people stepped out. They pulled a wire litter basket from the aircraft and hurried toward her.

"I'm glad to see you. Hawke splinted her leg and arm, but she's refusing to eat or drink. I know she has to be in pain." She led the two through the dining room and kitchen, into Leslie's bedroom.

The woman looked the same as she had the night before. Pale, her face pinched in pain. Only this morning her foot on the broken leg was swollen.

The Life Flight team checked her vital signs, asked questions Shandra didn't have the answers for, and lifted her onto the litter.

"We'll take her to the La Grande hospital," the female paramedic said.

"Thank you."

"I understand you're alone here. Will you be fine

until the search and rescue team arrives?" the pilot asked.

"Yes. I'm fine. Just take good care of Leslie." Shandra followed them to the airstrip and watched them take off.

Once they were out of sight she jogged back to the lodge, spread jam on a piece of bread, and went to the office. She flipped on the switches to the radio and contacted dispatch.

"Have you had any word from the helicopter about where Hawke and Ryan might be?" she asked.

"The helicopter is in the air and should be flying over the lodge soon. He'll fly different quadrants looking for them. I'll let you know when they contact me."

"Thank you." She turned off the radio to not run the batteries low. "But I won't be here to contact." She finished the bread, drank a glass of water, and filled up a water bottle. She spread more jam on two slices of bread, slapped them together and wrapped them up.

At the barn, she saddled up Queen, put the water and food in a saddlebag, and attached it to the back of her saddle. She found a camp shovel that folded up and tied it on the lacings behind the cantle.

She led the mare out of the barn and swung up into the saddle. Reining the horse to the beginning of the trail, she urged Queen into a trot.

~*~

Within an hour of Hawke saying they would catch up soon, he motioned for Ryan to stop and remain quiet. When Hawke dismounted, he did too. They tied the horses to a tree and continued on foot with Dog between them.

"He can't go any farther," Dani's voice carried through the trees.

"I said get up old man. If you'd told me where we were, you could have been rid of me yesterday." Rusk's voice sounded as if his patience was dangling by a thin wisp of spider's web.

Hawke motioned for Ryan to go to the right at two o'clock. Ryan understood they would come in from different directions, and hopefully, if Rusk had a gun that would keep him from shooting one of the hostages.

Ryan moved as slow and silently as he could through the underbrush to a two o'clock position. Just as cautiously, he moved toward the voices.

"He can't go anymore. If you hadn't hit him over the head, he'd not be holding you back." Dani's tone had become confrontational. He hoped they got there before Rusk hurt her.

Moments before Ryan made to step into the small clearing where the three stood, well, two stood and Clive leaned on Dani, Hawke stepped into view.

"Rusk, what are you doing with these people?" the State Trooper asked, his dog standing at his side with its hackles standing up and teeth bared.

Ryan eased out of the trees and brush now that the three had their backs to him.

"This old coot kept saying you'd find us. What are you some kind of Indian Medicine Man?" Rusk aimed a revolver at Hawke.

Ryan picked up speed. He pushed off with his right foot to leap at the man.

A stick snapped.

Rusk whipped around, the revolver in hand.

Before Ryan reached him, Dani knocked the hand

with the revolver down, grabbed his wrist, and put him in a debilitating hold.

Hawke had cuffs on Rusk by the time Ryan righted himself.

"Where did you learn that?" Hawke asked Dani with the first sign of respect he'd given the woman.

"Just because we fly planes doesn't mean we don't know hand to hand combat." She turned her attention to Clive. "Please tell me you have a horse for Clive to ride."

"We have a horse for each of you." Ryan led the way back to the horses. They put Clive on his horse, and Dani swung up onto Jack, Hawke's horse.

Hawke tied the parachute line to the handcuffs on Rusk and wrapped the other end around his wrist to keep the man from running off. With his shotgun, Hawke prodded Rusk along ahead of him.

"How long will it take us to get back to the lodge?" Dani asked.

"Two hours," Hawke said.

"We've been walking for hours. How can we be only two hours from the lodge?" Rusk asked in a whiny voice.

"You've been going in circles. That's what I couldn't understand." Hawke glanced over his shoulder at Clive. "Unless he was directing you."

Dani nodded. "He was. I thought it felt odd that we kept climbing but never came to the top of anything."

Hawke laughed. "Clive knows this country."

"I do," the man said from atop the horse.

~*~

Shandra slowed Queen to a walk after they passed through the meadow with the wildflowers. There would be no photos of flowers today. She craned her neck to the right, watching for the opening she'd discovered the last time they came this way.

"There!" She reined the mare to the right. They climbed up the gentle slope to the large granite bolder with a dark crease that looked like a sideways smile and the one lone tamarack tree beside it.

She dismounted and tied the horse to the tree. Shandra grabbed the shovel and made a circle around the boulder which was a good ten feet in diameter and four feet high. She stared at the ground looking for any freshly disturbed dirt.

When she didn't see any the first time around, she changed course and walked around it again. The different approach revealed a patch of plants that leaned rather than stood up straight. They also appeared less healthy.

Shandra unfolded the shovel and sunk the spade end into the ground. A mound of dirt, along with the puny looking plants, came up easily. Another shovelful, and she tapped something hard on the third thrust of the shovel into the hole. She tossed the tool to the side and dropped to her knees, digging in the dirt with her hands.

The first thing her fingers touched was rough. Removing the dirt around the object she extracted a canvas bundle the size of the pistols she'd witnessed in her dream. She untied the cord around the bundle and opened it. Two shiny silver pistols with pearl handles lay in her hands.

"I should have taken a photo." She refolded the canvas, retied the string and placed the weapons back in the hole. She pulled out her phone and took the photo. She'd take a photo of them unwrapped later.

With the pistols set to the side, she noticed what looked like tanned hide. Carefully, she removed the dirt around the leather bundle and took a photo before pulling it out and rolling it open. The elk bone breastplate lay on the flattened leather. She took a photo, rolled it back up and placed it by the canvas bundle.

The letters on the top of the wooden box spelled out Ammunition. Again, using care, she removed all the dirt around the box. She took a photo and worked the 10 x 14 inch box out of the hole. She took another photo. With shaking hands, the stubborn lid was hard to work loose. Inside, were small leather pouches with leather lacing around the tops drawing them closed. She snapped a picture of the bundles and picked one up. They were surprisingly heavy. Loosening the leather lacing, her eyes widened. She'd never seen gold in its raw state before. Judging from the weight, color, and the way the flakes glistened when the light hit them, she held gold in her hand.

Quickly, for fear someone who she didn't know would come upon her, she took a photo and placed the bag back in the box and replaced the lid.

The weapons and breastplate would fit in her saddlebags, but the box…

Chapter Sixteen

A mile from the lodge, Ryan was surprised to see a group of horseback riders being led by Fish and Wildlife State Trooper Sullen.

"What are you doing up here?" Hawke asked when he pulled Rusk to a stop in front of Sullen's horse's nose.

"We received a message from dispatch that you two went after hostages and required search and rescue." Sullen's gaze traveled to the man in handcuffs, Dani, and then Clive before drifting back to Hawke.

"Mrs. Greer must have got the radio working after we left," Hawke said.

Ryan grinned. He should have known she'd find a way to get a message out for help.

"She also asked for a Life Flight. It's been confirmed they picked up an older woman with two breaks and a concussion, but there was no mention of Mrs. Greer going with them. She's not at the lodge."

His gaze landed on Ryan.

"She wasn't at the lodge?" They had the only suspect they knew of in custody. Had someone come back and taken her? It made no sense.

"Don't get worried," Hawke said. "We'll figure it out when we get to the lodge."

It was easy for him to say, it wasn't his wife who was missing. Ryan was walking due to giving Clive his horse. He pushed through the search and rescue horses headed as fast as he could go toward the lodge.

He spotted the corral first. Maybe she'd decided to go for a ride. He leaned on the top corral rail and studied the horses. The mare she'd ridden twice wasn't here. Where would she go? The light came on at the same time as the others caught up to him.

"She went to that damn boulder," he said to Hawke.

"Let's get some fresh horses." Hawke dismounted and faced the other game warden. "Sullen, if Clive needs medical care take him with you and take the fellow in handcuffs. I'll be down tomorrow and write up my report. Book him for kidnapping right now. I'm sure it will be murder by the time I get down there."

"I didn't kill anyone," Rusk said.

"Hard to believe the way you pushed us around with that revolver," Dani said, dismounting. "I'll go with you to find Shandra."

"No," Hawke held up a hand. "You need to stay by the radio and transmit whatever it is Sullen needs done."

She scowled at him. "Just because this lunatic dragged us all over the mountain doesn't mean I'm incapable of riding a horse and finding my cousin."

"Did I say that?" Hawke stared at her. "I know you'd rather give orders than take them. Reporting on the radio is what needs done by someone who knows how to use it." Hawke faced Ryan. "Let's get those horses."

The search and rescue party followed a marching Dani to the lodge. They all disappeared inside.

"Is it really that important for her to stay here and man the radio?" Ryan asked.

"No. But you could see she was tired. We don't need her falling out of the saddle because she fell asleep to the rocking of the horse." Hawke walked in the barn and came back out with two lead ropes and halters. "I think the roan and the bay over there would be good choices."

Ryan nodded and took a halter and rope. He entered the corral and caught the bay.

They had the horses tied to the outside of the corral and were taking the saddles off the horses they'd ridden earlier when Dog barked and ran toward the far side of the landing strip.

Shandra on the black horse, Queen, walked out of the forest. She held something in front of her in the saddle.

"Hawke." Ryan tapped the other man on the arm and started toward her.

He met her halfway to the strip.

"What's in the box?"

"Who do the horses belong to?"

They spoke at the same time.

"They belong to Search and Rescue. You must have fixed the radio." He reached up for the box.

She shook her head. "This is the gold. We need to

get it in the barn."

He nodded and followed her across the open area to the barn.

Hawke had the doors open for her to ride in. "You found it," he said, taking the box from her and setting it on a larger wooden box.

"I did," she said, dismounting. She wrapped her arms around Ryan and hugged him. "I'm glad you're safe," she whispered.

He hugged her back and released her. "You, too."

She unbuckled her saddlebags and pulled out a canvas wrapped bundle and a leather wrapped bundle. "These are the other items."

Hawke took them, placing them on top of the box. "We have Rusk in custody. Sullen will be taking him down the mountain soon. Once he's gone, we'll give these to Dani."

Shandra nodded.

Ryan was glad the gold was found for Dani's sake, but they still didn't have the person who killed Doolie. "Do you think Rusk killed Doolie?"

Hawke didn't commit to a yes or a no. "We'll find out when they get him down the mountain and question him."

"Let's go let them know Shandra returned," Ryan said, taking her by the hand and leading her out of the barn.

It wasn't until they entered the lodge that he realized Hawke had stayed behind. Ryan wondered if he was staying away from Dani or he'd thought of the horses.

"Shandra!" Dani shot out of the chair and hurried across the great room. "I'm so glad you're okay. I don't know what I would have told our families if something had happened."

"I'm fine. I went for a horseback ride. It was better than sitting here worrying." She nodded to the State Trooper who had been to the lodge the other day.

"We're heading out," Trooper Sullen said. "Tell Hawke, I'll let him know when we get to the bottom and what we find out during questioning."

"Where's Clive?" Shandra asked, noticing the man wasn't in the room.

"I put him in the room Rusk was in. I think he has a concussion, but he refuses to go down with these guys and get medical attention." Dani waved a hand. "Men. They always think they know what's best."

Sullen shoved his hat on making ready to leave.

That's when Shandra realized. "Where is Rusk?"

Ryan stepped forward. "Yes, where is he?"

"I left Deputy Rainey on the porch with him." Sullen bolted for the door. Rusk was nowhere to be seen nor was the deputy.

Ryan ran to the end of the porch. "Rainey's here." He jumped off the end and raised up a slumping deputy.

Shandra ran to the barn.

Hawke was out cold with a gash on the side of his head in front of his horse's stall. Dog stood over him his teeth bared.

She glanced to where Hawke had put the box of gold. It was gone. The man couldn't get very far on foot with that heavy box. She snapped her fingers. And she knew where he was going.

Shandra hurried to the barn door. "Over here. He's knocked out Hawke."

The others came running. As more people entered

the building, the dog became more agitated.

"I think we'll need to clear out and let Hawke come to. That dog isn't going to let us near him," Ryan said, standing by Shandra. She nudged him and looked toward the empty spot where the box of gold had been. He nodded, telling her he realized what was missing and that Hawke would want to go after Rusk as soon as he came to.

Sullen ushered everyone out. He glanced over his shoulder. "Are you two staying?"

"Yeah. We'll make sure he's going to be okay when he comes around," Ryan said.

Shandra nodded. She would also search the barn to see if Hawke had hid the gold and other items.

"We'll form a posse to go after Rusk," Sullen said.

Shandra hated to leave the barn, but she had to give the map to the State Trooper. "I think I know where he's headed. I found a map in the room where he was staying. He had a trail mapped out to a red X." She led them back to the lodge. "I put it in the office." She ducked down the short hall to the office and picked up the map.

Dani stood at the end of the hall when she came out. "What do you have?"

"A map I found in Rusk's room after everyone left yesterday." Shandra handed it to Sullen. "That should give you a direction to look."

Dani shook her head. "As confused as he was yesterday, he's going to need that map to get him off the mountain."

"If Hawke weren't hurt—"

"Hawke's hurt?" Dani asked.

"It looks like Rusk caught him from behind with

123

something heavy," Sullen said. He held up the map. "I'll send half the team that direction and the rest of us will see if we can find his trail." He left and Shandra started out the door behind him.

Dani grabbed her shirt sleeve. "Do you need to bring Hawke in here?"

"We can't do anything until he comes to. His dog won't let us near him." Shandra pulled her shirt from her cousin's grasp.

"Oh. I'm going to check on Clive then clean up and go to bed. It's early, but I'm more tired than hungry. Help yourselves to whatever you can find in the kitchen."

"We will. Thank you. I'm glad they found you." Shandra gave the woman a hug and fled the lodge. She had to find out if Rusk had the gold or not.

Chapter Seventeen

Ryan sat on the box where Hawke had placed the gold and waited for the Trooper to come around.

Dog had remained by his owner's side. Voices outside the barn perked the dog's ears, but he kept his gaze locked on Ryan.

The sound of horse's hooves fading meant the search and rescue party had headed off to find Rusk. Ryan's stomach growled, catching the dog's attention.

The barn door burst open and Shandra charged in.

Dog raised up, his hackles standing once more.

"It's okay, I don't want to bother you or your human," Shandra said to the dog and stopped in front of Ryan. "We need to look around in here and see if Hawke hid the things I found."

"I did," came Hawke's muffled voice from the barn floor.

Shandra grinned at Ryan. "I knew it." She spun around and stopped when Dog growled.

"Down, Dog," Hawke said in a less than commanding tone.

The animal sat and the hair laid back down along his spine.

"Where's Rusk? I assume that's who hit me." Hawke slowly rose up and rolled to his back.

"We don't know," Ryan said, happy to see Hawke was coming around. They were going to need his tracking skills to find the man.

"We do know where he is going. That is if he can find the spot without his map," Shandra said. She told them how she'd found a map with the trails marked. "Trooper Sullen sent half the search and rescue party there, and he was going to look for tracks."

"I need to get up. He can't track his own horse." Hawke used the stall gate to pull himself to his feet. He leaned on the gate a few seconds and then cursed more than Ryan had heard him thus far.

"That son-of-a-bitch took Horse."

Ryan stared at the man. He'd been hit on the head harder than they'd thought. "Your horse is in that stall, the one you were laying in front of."

Hawke narrowed his eyes. "I know that's my horse, dammit. He stole my mule named Horse."

"You named your mule Horse?" Shandra asked.

"Yeah, I want him to act like a horse not like a stubborn mule. You know, you don't tell a child he's bad, then he thinks he is." Hawke peered at her as if what he said was a formula for the world's problems.

"Okay. It looks like Trooper Sullen will be following your mule. Named Horse," she said.

Ryan didn't care what the mule was called. They had a killer to catch, but they didn't have enough evidence. "When you searched his room, did you find anything else that might be evidence in his killing Doolie?"

Shandra shook her head. "He'd stripped the room of everything but the map. It was under the mattress."

"It doesn't make sense." Ryan sat back down on the wooden box by the stalls. "Did Rusk beat Doolie while trying to get the information about the gold out of him? If so, how did Rusk know about the gold?"

Hawke waved for Ryan to stand up. "Open that box and grab the gold and the other things. We need to get it in the house. I need a couple of those pills you were giving Leslie."

Ryan stood and lifted the lid on the box. There, under a burlap sack, sat the box of gold and the two bundles. Shandra picked up the bundles and he grabbed the gold. "Can you make it or do you want me to come back and help you?"

"I'll get there. Have Dani put those someplace safe. Not where they were before. We think Doolie moved them but it could have been someone else."

Ryan had wondered about that. If Doolie had been bludgeoned to discover where the gold was, he must not have known where it was hidden. But that didn't make sense if it were Doolie who had blabbed about it to Rusk at the tavern.

They entered the lodge and Dani came out of Rusk's room. The one where she'd put Clive.

"How's he doing?" Ryan asked.

"Getting more stubborn by the minute. I think Rusk hit him a little too hard and cracked his skull, but he refuses to let me fly him to a hospital." She shook her head. "I don't want him dying up here when he could have had attention at a medical facility."

Dani glanced at the objects they carried. "What do you have there?"

"Things we think Doolie stole and then hid to get later and sell." Ryan walked into the dining room. Shandra and Dani followed.

He placed the box on the table and opened the lid.

Dani picked up a leather pouch and opened it. Her eyes widened. "Is this what I think it is?"

"We'll know once you take it to an assayer," Ryan said.

Shandra unwrapped her two bundles. "I know this elk bone breastplate is worth a lot to collectors. The pistols, I don't know, but Doolie might have known their value."

Dani stared at the items. "Why would he steal these? The gold would have helped me keep this place going and given him a place to stay."

"Who knows why people do what they do. Maybe he was tired of living on the mountain and wanted to use this to set himself up somewhere else." Ryan plucked the pouch from Dani's hands and put the lid back on the box. "You need to hide this in case this is what Rusk was after and he comes back."

Dani nodded.

"And not where it was before. Even if he didn't take it from there, we aren't positive Doolie did either."

Shandra nodded to the cook's bedroom. "Is there somewhere in there to put it?"

"Let's see." Dani and Shandra rewrapped the pistols and breastplate and Ryan carried the box into the small bedroom.

"Under the floorboards would be the same as the

other room." Ryan said.

Dani smiled. "Then let's do the opposite, but not in this room." She strode out of the room, through the kitchen, and over to the corner in the great room where the ladder had been standing ever since their arrival.

Shandra stared up at the opening in the ceiling. "What have you been doing in this corner for so long?"

"The roofing had been loose here and caused water damage to this corner of the ceiling. I left the hole open to dry it out and I've been scraping off the rotted wood on the beams up here in hopes of having enough remaining that I can use some wood bond to fortify them and not have to tear the whole roof and ceiling off to put in new beams." She climbed the ladder, placed the bundle she had out of sight of the hole, took the one from Shandra and slid it in, then reached down for the box and set it up above, easing it slowly away from the hole.

Shandra wiped her hands together. That was done. They shouldn't have to worry about anyone getting their hands on that for a while.

Dani climbed down the ladder.

Ryan's stomach growled as Hawke walked through the front door.

"What took you so long to get in the house?" Ryan asked.

The trooper's face was paler than Shandra had ever seen it. She hurried to his side, helping him to the nearest chair.

"It's hard to walk when the world is spinning," Hawke said, easing down into the chair.

"What does that man use to hit people? Clive looked the same way when I found him," Dani said, placing a pillow behind Hawke's head where it leaned against the top of the chair.

"We were just going in the kitchen to get something to eat. Would you like me to bring you some tea and those pills?" Shandra asked.

Hawke's face scrunched. "Tea, as in what old ladies drink? No, thank you. Water, please."

"I'll grab that." She strode through the dining room and saw a flash of color in the cook's room.

Dani and Ryan came through the kitchen door. Shandra made a motion to keep talking, but waved for Ryan to go to the slightly open door.

She slipped into the bedroom but didn't see anything at first. There was only one place to hide. Shandra placed her hand on the edge of the cot.

A small slender body slipped out and made a run for the door. Facial features were petite, making her think it was a woman.

"Where did you come from?" Shandra asked, grasping at the person's arm. Her clothes were dirty, her athletic shoes scuffed and stained.

Ryan appeared in the doorway, catching the young woman's arms behind her back.

The stranger's glaring eyes settled on Shandra. But her lips remained in a firm tight line.

Dani appeared behind Ryan. "Let's see if Hawke knows who she is."

Ryan held onto the girl's arms and moved her out of the kitchen. Walking through the dining room, she struggled but must have realized he was too strong for her to get loose.

Shandra remembered the water and pills for the trooper. She hurried back to the kitchen for a glass of water and the bottle of pills. She returned to the great room in time for Hawke's statement, he didn't know who she was.

"Take her in and ask Clive," Shandra suggested.

The girl really started struggling. Shandra smiled. She knew Clive would know who she was. "I have a feeling Clive knows her."

The girl stopped struggling and glared at her.

"I think so, too." Ryan practically picked her up by her arms, forcing her across the floor to the room where Clive was recuperating.

Dani knocked on the door and opened it. "Clive, we need your assistance."

They all entered the room and the old wrangler's gaze latched onto the girl.

"Starla, what are you doing here?" he said.

"Starla who?" Ryan asked.

"That's Leslie's daughter from her first marriage." Clive sat up in bed. "Your momma's not here."

The young woman stopped fighting. "What happened to her?"

"We're not sure," Shandra stated and told her about finding the woman and her injuries.

"Why was she out there? And on a horse? She hates horses." Starla peered at Clive.

The old wrangler shrugged. "We don't know either. Did you just get here?"

She shook her head. "I've been here a week. Momma's been bringing me food to the cabin. When she hadn't come for a while, I came to see what was keeping her."

A week? Shandra wondered if the young woman had anything to do with her stepfather's death. "Why are you here?" she asked.

"I lost my job and had a fight with my boyfriend. Before he could beat me, I took off. I've been up here enough I know the trail. My friend gave me some food and a ride to the trailhead. I hiked in, and Momma's been feeding me and talking to me." Starla stared at Dani.

"You or your mother could have come to me. I wouldn't have kicked you out," Dani said.

The young woman shrugged. "She said you were new and had lots of rules. She wasn't sure you'd be as friendly about me being here as Uncle Charlie always was."

Ryan released her wrists. "Did you see the helicopter take your mom away earlier today?" he asked.

"I saw the Life Flight, but didn't know it was Momma. I began to wonder when she didn't come to see me like she'd been doing right before lunch."

Shandra realized that was why the cook had been so evasive the day they'd found the body about where she'd been during the time Doolie was killed. She'd probably been with Starla.

"You can stay in the cabin for now. I don't have anyone booked for a week or so. We'll figure out what to do after that."

"If I don't get back on my feet right away, she can wrangle. She's gone on enough rides with me to not get people lost," Clive said.

"We'll see," Dani said.

Ryan's stomach growled.

"I'll go make food for everyone," Shandra said. She glanced at the young woman. "Why don't you come help me?"

Starla glanced at Dani. "Is that okay?"

Dani nodded.

"Come on. We'll set food out in the dining room," Shandra said over her shoulder. On the way through the great room she told Hawke the newcomer was Leslie's daughter.

He opened an eye and studied her as they walked by.

She wondered if he was trying to decide if the slip of a woman could wield the stick they'd found hard enough to do the damage to Doolie's skull.

In the kitchen, she put Starla to work making sandwiches while Shandra found a container of cookies and instant lemonade mix. She pumped the handle of the old-fashioned water faucet and asked, "Where does this water come from?"

"It's piped in from a spring that's north of the lodge. Uncle Charlie was pretty proud of his 'running' water." The girl smiled.

"It sounds like you have fond memories of him." Shandra stirred the drink.

"He was kind of crude but you knew who he liked and who he didn't. He didn't pretend. Even with people who stayed here." She scowled.

"Does someone pretend to like you?" Shandra asked.

Starla peered at the bread in her hand, the hand with the knife and peanut butter stalled as well. "Doolie, my stepdad, he would pat me on the head and smile at me, but it never felt genuine. It was more as if he tolerated me."

"Was he here when you arrived?" Shandra had an

idea that maybe learning what had happened up to them arriving at the lodge would help to figure out who killed the man.

"Yeah. He and Dani, the new owner, got into an argument. He called her some awful names." Starla shuddered. "I would have broken down and bawled if someone talked to me that way."

"She's tough. Comes from telling men what to do in the Air Force."

Starla slapped the bread on the counter. "The Air Force? Really?"

"Yes. She went through the Air Force Academy and became an officer." Shandra was proud of Dani, not only for being a woman who pursued her dreams of being in the Air Force, but also for their heritage, even though she could tell Dani preferred that part of her wasn't apparent.

"She must be really smart." Starla picked the slice of bread back up and finished spreading the peanut butter.

"She is. I'm sure you are, too. And brave. I'm not sure I could have followed the right trails to the hunting lodge by myself."

"I'm used to doing things on my own. The last ten years, Momma and Doolie have worked up here from May to November. I've lived with relatives and friends to finish school." She slapped two spread slices together and worked on another set.

"Really? They left you to fend for yourself? You *are* braver than me." Shandra wondered at the maternal instincts of a woman who left her daughter to others and when she was in pain from two broken bones worried about gold.

"After you arrived, did you ever see your mom and Doolie talking?" Shandra wanted to find out if the two had conspired to steal the gold.

"They had a big argument right before Doolie left. You know after he called Dani all those names and she told him to leave." She shook her head. "He'd been drinking a lot since Uncle Charlie died. I know they were good friends but he seemed angry. As if he were mad that Uncle Charlie left him."

It always amazed Shandra how youth could be so insightful without knowing it.

Chapter Eighteen

Ryan wandered into the dining room to see what was taking the 'cooks' so long. Plates and silverware had been set out along with a plate of peanut butter and jelly sandwiches and a bowl of chips.

His stomach rumbled again, but he crept up to the kitchen door. The sound of two conversing voices made him smile. Shandra was the only person he knew who could gain anyone's trust. Be it a young person or a killer.

He shook his head and went back to the table and sat down, putting a sandwich and handful of chips on his plate.

The kitchen door opened and the two walked out. Shandra carried a pitcher of water in one hand and a pitcher of lemonade in the other. Starla had a tray of glasses.

"I wondered when your stomach would bring you in here," Shandra said. She placed the pitchers on the table and turned to the young woman. "Starla, this is my husband, Ryan Greer."

Starla nodded her head. "I'd say pleased to meet you, but you had me in a hold like you're a policeman or something."

"You've had experience with the police?" he asked.

She didn't answer, making him think she probably had.

"Starla why don't you sit down and eat. I'll get Dani and see if Hawke is up to anything after taking those pills." Shandra walked out of the room.

Ryan motioned to the bench across the table. "Have a seat. I don't bite and I won't ask questions."

She studied him a moment before taking a seat on the opposite side of the table on the opposite end.

He slid the plate of sandwiches her way and shoved the potato chip bowl. She caught the dish before it dropped off the end of the table. "Good catch," he said, getting him a surprised look from Starla.

Shandra returned with Dani. His wife sat down beside him. Her cousin took a spot across the table from them. She glanced at Starla sitting on the end of the bench but didn't comment.

"Are we any closer to finding out who killed Doolie?" Dani asked.

Starla's intake of breath made him wonder if she hadn't known he was dead. But that didn't make sense considering all that had been going on around here.

Both women glanced at Starla. She stared at the plate of food in front of her.

"I'm going to see if we can contact the State Police and see what they've come up with so far." Ryan grabbed another sandwich and kissed the top of Shandra's head. "I'll grab grumpy and see if we can get some answers."

As he went through the door Starla asked, "Who is Grumpy?"

He grinned and walked over to where the State Trooper sat with his eyes closed. Dog lay on the floor at his feet. "Are you in any shape to help me contact your guys and see what we can find out so far about the evidence we sent them?"

"Point me in the right direction, and I'll vouch for you." Hawke eased himself to the edge of the chair and stood. He wobbled a bit then started forward motion. "If that damn woodpecker in my head doesn't quit hammering away, I'm going to go crazy."

"It goes away with time." Ryan remembered all the times he'd had his bell rung. It wasn't fun at the time or for days afterwards.

"I know. The first time I had it happen I was bucked off a horse. Tried to be a big rodeo cowboy in high school. It's about as safe as this job." Hawke walked into the office and sank onto the floor beside the desk as there was only one chair in the room. Dog lay across his lap.

"You good?" Ryan asked him.

"Yeah. Just hand me the mic when they want to talk to me."

Ryan sat in front of the radio and dialed in the frequency Hawke told him. Dispatch put him through to the State Police Headquarters in La Grande.

"This is Ryan Greer, I'm a detective from Idaho. I'm here with Fish and Wildlife State Trooper Hawke who has a head injury. But he's willing to talk to whoever to get information that will help us investigate the death that occurred at Charlie's Hunting Lodge in the Wallowa Mountains."

"This is Hawke's supervisor, Lieutenant Titus."

Ryan handed the mic down to Hawke.

"Sir, I'm in no shape to read anything or write it down. I'll give my book to Greer, and if you have questions, he can find the answers. And give him any information that has come up on the case." Hawke handed the mic back to Ryan.

"Since you haven't been in to type up any formal information, I'll refrain from having Greer read me your whole notebook. What I can tell you is the coroner has determined the death was due to multiple strikes to the head. The stick you sent down with the body is the murder weapon. The wood was too porous to get any prints. They are working on possibly getting epithelial samples and possible DNA but that takes weeks. The first swing knocked him to the ground and according to the forensic specialist was the initial blow that killed him. The others make this seem as if it wasn't a thought-out plan but more like something triggered the rage that the other blows portray."

"So, whoever did this would have bloody clothes to get rid of?" Ryan asked.

"Yes. The coroner said there would be no way blood didn't spatter on the assailant. Either shoes while they stood over the body striking the blows or the initial one that broke open the scalp."

"Did you ever find out who this Harris Rusk is?" Ryan asked.

"He's an individual from our area who lends money on collateral. From what we've found out so far,

Doolie Lincoln had a loan with him for forty thousand dollars. He put up the hunting lodge as collateral."

"That's why Rusk is so desperate to get something from here. He's discovered Doolie didn't own the lodge and wants paid." Ryan now understood the man's desperation but not why he would knock out Clive, take Dani hostage, and then hit Hawke.

"Thank you for the information, Lieutenant. Rusk was captured, but he got away again by knocking two people over the head. Search and Rescue are out looking for him now. We'll let you know when we hear from Sullen and the Search and Rescue. You might want to have someone stand guard over the woman, Leslie Lincoln, who was flown out of here this morning. She's a person of interest as well."

"I already have a guard on her room. She *is* the spouse of the murder victim." The lieutenant signed off.

Ryan turned the system off to save the battery and helped Hawke to his feet. "I think Shandra and I will check the clothing of the people who live and work at the lodge."

"That's a good idea," Hawke said as they slowly walked down the hall and back to the great room.

The three women were seated.

He placed Hawke back in a cushioned chair and faced the women. "We've been on the radio with the State Police. Shandra and I are going to search your room," he said to Dani. "Leslie's room and…" He glanced at Starla, "the cabin you've been staying in. Which one is it?"

She glared at him.

"Then I guess we'll check all three of them." He held out a hand to Shandra. "Dani, would you make sure Starla stays in this room until we've checked everywhere?"

She nodded, but he could tell she wasn't happy to be in the category of a suspect.

Hawke stirred. "My pack in the barn has a blood test kit."

"I'll get it if we come up with anything promising," Ryan said.

When they stepped into Dani's room, Shandra asked, "What did they have to say that we are invading my cousin's privacy?"

He told her about the blood spatter.

She opened the drawers and looked over each piece of clothing. "You know we aren't going to find any blood on Dani's clothes. She'd never let the words of a drunk send her into enough of a rage to kill him."

Ryan shrugged. "We don't know if she has PTSD or what her boundary is for full on rage. Maybe all of those years putting up with it from the officers above and below her, she finally cracked." He found her shoes and checked them for any dark stains.

"She's too together for that to happen." Shandra closed the bottom drawer. "Nothing in there looked stained." She took down the jackets and coats hanging on hooks by the door. "Nothing here either. I say we go to Leslie's room. She has the most motive."

"True." He hadn't found anything that resembled a spatter of blood on the clothing in Dani's dirty clothes basket.

They walked out of the hall and Shandra gave Dani a thumbs up.

Ryan hid a grin. His wife may have only found out about her cousin four days ago, but she was already pulling for her in all ways a family member does. That's what he loved about Shandra. For having grown up an only child in a family that tolerated her, she had grasped her paternal family's roots with gusto and believed in every single one of them.

They moved through the dining room and kitchen into the cook's quarters. Shandra went straight to the dirty clothes basket. She dug all of the clothes out and called him over. "What do you think that is?"

The brownish stains on the bottom of the clothes bin could have been from blood. "I'll get the test kit from Hawke's pack while you keep looking."

Shandra waved him off and began going through the woman's clothes in the drawers. Everything was neat, tidy, and clean. She looked over the sweater, jacket, and coat hanging on a hook by the door. She didn't see anything incriminating on them. But if there had been something with blood on it how would she get rid of the garment?

She stepped out of the room and knew how the item could have been dealt with. Shandra walked over to the wood cookstove. The stove hadn't been used since Hawke started it to heat water for tea for Leslie. Even though he'd told her to keep it going, she'd seen no need to worry about it once Leslie was Air Flighted out. She opened the door to the fire box and dug around with the poker, moving charcoaled wood, ashes, and debris. The acrid smell of debris and tang of pine tickled her nose. Something metal clanged when she moved the poker.

"What are you doing?" Ryan asked when he walked into the room.

"Looking for evidence."

He walked on by and into the cook's quarters.

Shandra found a baking tray and pulled all the ash and charred pieces of wood out onto the tray. When the fire box was empty, she carried the tray to the table.

Ryan stepped out of the small bedroom. "It is blood. I took a photo of it and will bag it as evidence." He walked over. "What are you doing?"

"If you were a cook who used a wood burning stove, where would you get rid of bloody clothing?"

"Good point." Ryan returned to the room.

Shandra dug through the ashes and charred pieces looking for the metal she'd heard. The poker struck something. She grabbed a basting brush and swept at the ashes until the metal button from a pair of jeans appeared.

Ryan returned with a paper evidence bag. "Did you find something?"

"Maybe. Why would a metal button from a pair of jeans be in a wood cookstove?" She pointed to the shiny object.

"I guess we'll find out." Ryan took a photo of the button, then bagged it as evidence.

Shandra continued to brush the ashes around. "I think these little things are the metal teeth in a zipper." She'd found six little square metal pieces.

He bagged them. "We still need to go check out the cabin."

She nodded. "I want to see if the pants in Leslie's room have buttons that match." Her enthusiasm for finding the button waned when she saw the cook's jeans. They were the style older women wore with an elastic waist. There wasn't a button or zipper on a single pair.

Ryan stood by Hawke's chair talking low when she entered the great room.

Shandra shot a glance to the two women. They were both wearing denim jeans. It was Dani's lodge. She could have put the pants in the stove just as easily as Leslie. Same with Starla, seeing how she knew how to get in through the open kitchen window.

She didn't want to find out the button came from one of Dani's pants. She'd decided to wait until they'd checked out the cabin before checking her cousin's jeans for the button.

"Are you ready?" she asked Ryan.

He nodded and followed her outside. "What did you find?"

"Leslie wore elastic waist jeans. No buttons or zippers." She walked to the first cabin and opened the door. The interior was dusty and didn't show any sign of anyone having stayed in it recently. She closed the door and moved to cabin two. This cabin was the same.

"Must be lucky number three," Ryan said, stepping around her and opening the door.

Jackpot.

The bed was made, a plastic garbage bag was folded on the top of the chest of drawers. On the bureau, folded nicely, were different sizes of various types of clothing. Men's, women's, children's. The clothing reminded her of a lost and found box at a church or school.

She stared at Ryan. "That's what it is."

"What?" He had been looking under the bed.

"This mismatch of clothing. These are the lost and found clothing that people leave behind. Leslie must have given them to Starla. From what she told me,

Starla came here with nothing but food a friend had given her."

He stood. "Then there is no way to match the button to anything she has."

"True. But if we rule out Dani…then the jeans would have had to come from here." She waved a hand over the clothing.

"You are forgetting there was one other person here."

Chapter Nineteen

As much as Ryan hated to pin this on Clive, given
the man was injured. He was still very much a suspect.
"We need to go check out Clive's jeans in the
bunkhouse."

Shandra nodded.

He led the way, opening the door and realizing this
had been a bachelor's home for thirty years. The odors
of leather, old socks, and wood smoke hung in the air.
The furnishings were sparse. A table, four chairs, wood
stove and two sets of bunk beds. Old army issue trunks
sat at the ends of the bunks and one at the side of the
head of the bottom bunks.

The one closest to the door and stove was Clive's.
He could tell by the worn quilt and wool blanket that
the bed was used often. The other lower bunk had a
sleeping bag spread across it and what looked like
Hawke's saddlebag on the trunk.

Shandra pointed to the stove. "He wouldn't need to

take the jeans to the kitchen to burn."

Ryan agreed. "Let's check anyway." He opened the trunk beside Clive's bed. The contents were clothes and mementos. He held up a pair of jeans.

Shandra inspected the button. "That's not the same."

"That leaves Dani or the clothing Starla is using." Ryan opened the door and they walked back to the lodge.

The sound of voices and creak of leather caused him to stop and look around. Horses and riders approached from the north, State Trooper Sullen led the group of Search and Rescue riders.

Ryan was pleased to see Rusk riding Hawke's mule.

Shandra touched his arm. "I'm going to check the jeans in Dani's room."

He nodded and walked out to meet the search party. "I see you found him."

Sullen shook his head. "He walked into us. I've never seen someone who can get so turned around in the forest."

"To my credit, everything out here looks the same," Rusk said.

Ryan laughed. "Just don't let him near Hawke. He's still not feeling good after this guy coldcocked him." Ryan glared at Rusk. "And he's not happy you took his mule."

"We'll put him in the barn with two guards," Sullen said, reining his horse toward the corral.

Ryan entered the lodge as Shandra walked down the hall. From her downcast eyes, she'd found out who wore the type of jeans that had been burned.

147

"The Search and Rescue team just rode in. Dani can you and Starla get some dinner put together? They'll spend the night and head out in the morning with Rusk."

"They got him? Good!" Dani's show of emotion proved she didn't like the man. Was it because she already knew he'd come here to repossess the lodge or was it because he'd hurt Clive?

"Come on Starla, I believe we can pull together a big pot of spaghetti." Dani herded the younger woman toward the dining room and kitchen.

Shandra walked over to him.

"What do you want to do?" he asked, putting an arm around her shoulders.

"I'm not sure. I mean there could have been a reason for her burning a pair of jeans in the cookstove, right?" Shandra peered at him with hope in her eyes.

"There could be a reasonable explanation, but we also have to continue to consider her a suspect." He hated to tell her that, but he couldn't lie to her.

"What are you two talking about?" Hawke asked, stirring in the chair and sitting up straighter.

Ryan revealed to him all that they'd discovered while looking for blood spattered clothing.

"I hate to say it, but she's been at the top of my list. Clive told me that there had been more than one argument between Doolie and Dani since the reading of Charlie's will." He ran a hand over his face. "Take it from me, whether you're a half-breed or all American Indian, having someone else call you half-breed or Injun enough times and you take to hating them as much as if they'd called you a mother-fucker."

Shandra bristled in Ryan's arm. "Is that what

Doolie called her?"

"Among other things I won't repeat. Doolie was a mean drunk. Nice, likable person when he was sober, but the alcohol made him mean as a snorting bull." Hawke winced and rose to his feet. "You said Sullen was back?"

"Yes. But you stay out of the barn." Ryan put a hand on the man's chest.

"What about my mule?" Hawke narrowed his eyes.

"I'll go check on him," Shandra said. "Does he like women? He won't growl at me like your dog?"

Hawke grinned. "He'll be fine for you. Just don't turn your back on him."

"I'll go with her." Ryan clasped Shandra's hand and led her out of the lodge. Sullen and several others were headed their way.

Ryan stopped when they were abreast of the State Trooper. "Hawke's in a better mood. You can bring him up to speed. He's worried about his mule. Afraid Rusk might have harmed it."

"Good luck checking on that ornery thing. I'm surprised Rusk stayed on him." Sullen thought a minute. "You know, I think that mule brought Rusk to us. Rusk was yanking on the reins, trying to get the mule to turn. The animal just kept heading right straight for us."

"You have Rusk handcuffed and tied?" Ryan asked.

"He's not getting away this time." Sullen's face was a mask of determination.

"Good." Ryan continued to the barn.

"Are we going to talk to Rusk?" Shandra asked.

"If he acts like he'll talk." Ryan opened the barn

door and entered.

A deputy stood, then sat back down when he saw who'd entered.

"Hawke was worried about his mule," Ryan said, walking over to the stall where Hawke had noticed his mule was missing. He grabbed the halter and lead rope on the gate and they walked back out to the corral.

The tall bay colored mule stood by the gate. As if he knew he belonged in the barn and not with the other horses.

"Let me," Shandra said. She took the halter and Ryan opened the corral gate.

Shandra slipped in, walking slowly to the mule. He ducked his large head, and she put the halter on him. His big nose was velvety soft. "You're a good boy. I think you are a hero for bringing that nasty Rusk back to us." She kissed the side of his face and led him out of the corral.

She'd had little experience with mules. Her stepfather hadn't liked them, so there had been none on the ranch. But she'd always marveled at their strength but awkward looks.

Ryan opened the barn door and she led the tall creature inside.

The mule's gaze went to Rusk and he snorted.

"It's okay. He's not going to bother you again." Shandra pet the mule's muzzle and continued to the stall next to Hawke's horse.

Ryan was ahead of her and opened the stall gate. Horse walked in, placing his head over the rails between the two stalls. The appaloosa gelding walked over. They stood nostril to nostril conversing until Shandra parted them to get the halter off.

"I'll give you some extra grain," she said to the mule and walked out, keeping her back to the gate. He seemed like he had good manners but Hawke had warned her, and she figured there was a reason.

With the gate locked, she and Ryan fed the horse and mule hay and grain.

The deputy and another man sat, straddling the wooden box Hawke had hid the gold in earlier that day. The two men were on either end with playing cards on the space between them.

She scanned the barn and found Rusk. His hands were handcuffed behind him and around a barn post.

Ryan walked over to within about eight feet of him. "Right now, we have you for assault of an officer and assault on Clive. Also horse theft."

"I'm sure around here horse theft is a longer sentence than the assaults," Shandra said, having read that at one time in a trivia book. But she wasn't sure if the state had been Oregon or another one.

"But when we find the evidence that you killed Doolie—"

"I didn't kill him. We had a talk. He said he'd meet me the next day with what he owed me. He didn't show," Rusk said, his eyes jittered in the sockets.

"We know you were the last person to see him before he died." Ryan crossed his arms.

"I was not. When I started around the end of the bunkhouse, I heard a woman's voice." Rusk stared at Ryan. "That's the truth."

"How did Doolie plan to pay you back the forty grand?" Ryan asked him.

Shandra hadn't heard about the sum of money Doolie owed. She studied the man. She'd thought he'd looked like he was casing the lodge inventory and it sounded like he had been.

"How do you know about that?" Rusk asked.

"Same way we know you met Doolie about a mile away from here and followed him." Ryan raised an eyebrow.

"Why would you follow him if you had made plans to meet the next day?" Shandra asked.

Rusk glanced from Ryan to Shandra to Ryan and back to her. "I thought you were newlyweds? You act an awful lot like cop partners."

"We are newlyweds," Shandra said. "And we are partners." She wasn't going to let him think she wasn't law enforcement.

"We have the murder weapon. Why'd you pick up that limb and hit Doolie?" Ryan stared at Rusk. "You didn't hit him once. You hit him multiple times. Were you trying to get him to tell you where you'd find the money?"

"No! I said I didn't kill him. When we met, he said he'd hidden something that would cover what he owed me, but there were guests at the lodge and he couldn't get to it. I followed him because I didn't believe him. Even drunk, he'd realized I was behind him. He swung a limb at me and missed. He landed on the ground. I told him he'd better meet me the next day with my money or I'd tell the new owner that the place was going to me."

Shandra's heart landed in her throat. Had Dani heard this conversation and in a rage over Doolie having given away her family's legacy, she killed him?

"Do you remember what the woman's voice sounded like?" she asked.

"A woman." He stared at her like she'd asked a stupid question.

"Did it sound old, young, mature. High pitched, gravelly, monotone."

He continued to stare at her. "I don't know. It was a woman. It wasn't deep like a man's."

They had three female suspects with Dani being on the top of the list of three.

Chapter Twenty

Shandra was impressed with the spaghetti feed her cousin and Starla pulled together for the Search and Rescue crew and everyone else at the lodge.

"That was good, and on such short notice," Shandra said, helping the other two clear the table.

Dani smiled. "When I grumbled about having to put together impromptu meals for officers because I was the only female, I didn't know it would come in handy as the owner of a hunting lodge."

The kitchen was warm and the windows had been thrown open to allow the heat to escape.

Shandra understood how the meal had been pulled together so easily. Empty jars of spaghetti sauce sat on the counter along with several boxes that had held the noodles.

"Put those in the sink and pump in some water. I'll get some hot water going on the stove." Dani picked up the boxes and shoved them into the cookstove along with another chunk of firewood.

Shandra pumped the handle on the water faucet and asked, "What do you do with your trash?"

Starla returned from the dining room with another load of dishes. She placed them on the drainboard.

Dani said, "The jars are washed out and used to store things in the pantry."

That made sense given they would have to haul all the garbage out. "And cans and paper?"

"Cans are rinsed and crushed. When we get a bin full, I haul it down to the valley. Anything burnable goes in here or the woodstove in the bunkhouse." Dani shoved a large pot of water to the back of the stove.

"Like paper, boxes, clothing?" Shandra was hoping her cousin would admit to putting the pair of pants in the cookstove.

Dani studied her. "Were you the one digging around in the stove? I thought someone had been nice and cleaned out the ashes."

"Did you have a reason to burn a pair of pants in the stove?" Shandra asked.

"Yes, I did. They were a worn-out pair with tar on them and I'd caught them on nails while crawling around fixing the roof." She tapped her fingers on the table. "I think it was about a week or so ago that I put them in there."

"How often do the ashes get cleaned?" Shandra sprinkled dish soap in the water.

"They need to be emptied every other day to keep a good fire burning, but Leslie wasn't one to do more than she had to. She usually only took one can of ash out." Dani grabbed a towel and grasped the handle on the pot of steaming water. She poured half the water into the sink and placed the pot beside it. "This is to rinse."

"If you want to put the food away, I'll wash the dishes," Starla offered.

Dani nodded and shoved a tea towel in Shandra's hands. "You can rinse and dry."

Left at the sink helping with the dishes, she watched Dani. The woman didn't act as if she were a suspect in a murder. She'd matter-of-factly told how the pants came to be in the stove.

It was all plausible, but why hadn't they found the clothing with the stains when there had been blood in Leslie's basket… "How do you do laundry around here? You must have to wash sheets for the guest beds and your own clothing."

"Behind the shower house is an old wringer washing machine. We have to do the laundry the old-fashioned way." Dani poured the leftover spaghetti in a jar and screwed on the lid.

"What do you do with that to keep it cool?" Shandra had noticed there wasn't a refrigerator in the kitchen.

"There's a spring house cellar under the lodge." Dani handed her the jar of sauce and picked up the bowl of butter that had been on the table for their bread. "Follow me."

They walked through the dining room, down the hall, out the backdoor, and over to a door in the ground that went under the kitchen. Dani handed her the bowl of butter and grasped the door handle, heaving it open.

Wooden stairs descended into a dark hole.

"How do you see where to go?" Shandra trusted her cousin, but at the same time this looked like a great place to leave someone to die.

Dani stuck her hand alongside the door opening and brought out a camping lantern. Attached to the handle was a propane lighter. She lit the lantern, retrieved the bowl of butter and descended the stairs.

Shandra followed, watching that her head and hand didn't touch cobwebs. The air was cool and damp. The sweetness of apples and gamey smell of wild meat faintly scented the air as they stepped on the dirt floor. A metal pipe along the ceiling dripped water.

"That's the water that's piped from the spring. Being underground like this and having the spring water helps keep the temperature constant down here." Dani placed the butter under a glass cover like a cake cover. She took the jar from Shandra and placed it on a shelf with other canned goods. "This is pretty antiquated, but up here you have no choice."

"This is like our ancestors lived," Shandra said.

Dani shook her head. "This is better than they lived."

Shandra studied her cousin in the lantern light. "I never knew my father's family until I grew older. They were kept from me. What about you?"

Dani hung the lantern from a hook on a beam only inches from their heads. "I was lucky. My father wanted more and left the reservation after high school. He got a degree and married well. We visited family, but I was never really a part of anything they did."

"Do you regret it?" It was an odd place to be having this conversation, but the two of them had never really had a chance to talk about family since Shandra had arrived.

"Yes and no. My life has been everything I've

wanted." She scowled. "With a few minor bumps along the way. But there have been times, when people called me half-breed and Injun that I wondered if I had been brought up knowing my culture if I'd be proud of those names or still feel dirty."

"I was saved most of the name calling because my stepfather insisted I use his last name and never speak of being half Indian. Reconnecting with my family has brought me so much joy and insight into who I am. You might want to try it." Shandra put an arm around Dani's shoulders and gave her a hug. "I know it has helped me discover more of my strength."

Dani unhooked the lantern. "Come on. Starla's going to think we left all the dishes to her."

"She's a good kid. Maybe you could use her here, until her mother is able to work again."

Dani shook her head. "I like Starla, but we don't know if she killed Doolie. She was here at the time. And as for Leslie…she's not coming back. She's been lazy and insolent. I only kept her because Doolie asked me to." She sighed. "I sure hope you find out who killed him. I don't like walking around thinking someone might do the same to me." She motioned for Shandra to climb the stairs first.

Her words sounded sincere and that she felt she could potentially be the next victim. That didn't sound like the words of someone who had bludgeoned anyone in a state of rage.

Dani turned out the lantern, hung it up, and they closed the door.

"Show me the washing machine," she said, still wondering about the stains in Leslie's clothes basket.

~*~

Ryan, along with Hawke and Sullen, convened in the office after the meal and radioed dispatch to patch them through to their superior. Once the State Police Lieutenant was filled in on what they had so far, they listened to the new information that had been gathered off the mountain.

"Mrs. Lincoln is doing better and insisting she needs to get back to work," the lieutenant said.

"She just has unfinished business up here," Hawke replied.

Ryan studied Hawke. "What unfinished business?"

"Shandra said when I'd gone to get the sticks to splint her breaks, the woman woke up asking about the gold." Hawke rubbed a hand over his chin. "Maybe we need to let her come back up here."

"Do you think she killed Doolie?" Ryan believed the woman had the hatred for the man, but could she have had the physical strength to cause the blows?

"I believe she and Dani had the most to gain from Doolie's death." Hawke held his hands up as if weighing something in them.

"Shandra isn't going to like that you believe Dani could have done this." Ryan had seen the connection growing between the two cousins.

"Sometimes we don't know people as well as we think." Hawke grasped the microphone. "If the doctor is okay to release Mrs. Lincoln, let her go. If she comes up here, we will watch her."

"I thought she was a suspect?" the lieutenant asked.

"She is. But we are having trouble getting the evidence we need."

"I can send the blood sample I took from the clothes hamper down with Sullen tomorrow. If it's

Doolie's blood that will start our evidence against her."
Ryan was glad they had someone to investigate besides
Dani.

Sullen stood. "Where is this blood sample?"

"I'll get it. I put it in Hawke's saddlebag with the
other items we found." Ryan said, opening the office
door.

"I'll go with you. I'm feeling better and want to
make sure Jack and Horse are okay." Hawke and Dog
exited the room behind the other two.

The three men walked out of the lodge and toward
the barn.

Ryan caught a glimpse of someone behind the
shower house. "I'll catch up to you."

He walked down to the end of the lodge and over
to the shower house. He looked around the corner and
found Dani and Shandra talking about an antiquated
washing machine. "What are you two doing out here?"

They both startled. Dani cursed under her breath
and Shandra spun toward him.

"You! That's not nice sneaking up on people,"
Shandra had her hands over her heart.

"I didn't mean to sneak up. We were headed to the
barn and I saw movement over here." He glanced at
Dani and then his wife. "With all that's gone on around
here, I was being cautious."

"I don't blame you," Dani said. "I need to get back
in and help Starla." She headed around the shower
house.

"What were you two talking about?" Ryan grasped
Shandra's hand to lead her away.

"This is how they wash the sheets and clothing
here." Shandra released his hand and walked over to a

bucket sitting under a faucet. The pipe came from the tank on top of the shower house. "Look in this bucket."

He walked over and noticed the water had a brownish tint and yellow jackets were hanging around the rim. "Did you ask Dani about this?"

"She said that Leslie would soak things that were extra dirty." She raised her eyebrows. "And that looks like old bloody water to me."

Ryan pulled out his phone. "Find something I can dig the clothing out with." He took photos of the bucket.

Shandra only walked a few steps away and returned with a paddle. "She said this is used to stir the clothing."

Grasping the paddle in both hands, he dipped it in the bucket, aggravating the yellow jackets, and lifted the garment out.

Shandra started to reach for the clothing.

"Don't touch. Go to the barn and get Sullen or Hawke. These need to be put some place to dry and be bagged as evidence. But it has to dry where no one can tamper with the overalls."

Chapter Twenty-one

Shandra ran to the barn and threw the door open. "Hawke, Sullen!"

They both hurried forward. Hawke from near his horses and Sullen from over by Rusk.

"What's wrong?" Hawke asked.

"We found something. Evidence we think." She gulped air and leaned close to Hawke, whispering, "It's clothing in a bucket of water."

He nodded. "Sullen, bring the blood test kit."

They exited the barn together.

"Where did you find this?" Sullen asked.

"I was asking Dani about how things run around here and where people washed their clothes. She took me over to see the wringer washing machine. I noticed a bucket filled with water had yellow jackets hanging around the rim. I glanced at the reddish-brown water and then kept Dani away. Ryan arrived and Dani went back in the lodge." Shandra led them up to where Ryan stood by the bucket. The paddle extended from the bucket.

"Did Shandra tell you what we found?" he asked.

"Yes." Sullen set down the kit he'd been carrying, wiggled his hands into latex gloves, and pulled out a small glass jar with a stopper.

Ryan used the paddle to pick up the clothing and drop water into the jar Sullen held. When the finger sized jar was half full, the trooper opened an ampule, sprinkling the contents into the water. He shook the little jar and the liquid turned blueish-green.

"It's blood."

"These clothes will need to dry so you can bag them without compromising the evidence," Ryan said.

Hawke waved to the bunkhouse. "All of Search and Rescue will be in there tonight. Can't think of a safer place to keep the suspects away. We can hang the clothes up to dry and bag it in the morning before Sullen leaves."

"Let's take the bucket and all." Sullen handed the test kit to Ryan and grasped the handle of the bucket with his gloved hand.

The three headed off to the bunkhouse.

Shandra glanced around. She wasn't sure she wanted to go back in the house. Dani may ask what took her so long. If she went for a walk, then she could say, that's what she did.

Finding the path behind the corral was easy. She set out at a stroll, enjoying the different scents of the forest in the evening as compared to the heat of the day. The decaying leaves of the forest floor and pine scent were muted. A crispness that could only be felt as the sun went down in the evening and came up at dawn, tingled the hair on her bare arms.

Before she knew it, darkness had seeped through the trees, making it hard for her to see the path. "I should have gone in the lodge and not been such a chicken," she said to herself, wondering if it would be closer to turn around and go back or keep going.

"Ryan is going to be upset," she said, knowing she should have thought about the time.

Standing in one spot, she thought she heard something walking toward her. It wasn't footsteps but the sound of leaves on the ground scrunching. Unsure if it could be a predator, human or animal, she decided to face her visitor. If it turned out to be an animal, she'd yell loud enough to hopefully scare the creature away. If it turned out to be an unfriendly human, she hoped she could figure out an escape.

She pivoted in time to see something trotting along the path. "Dog?" she asked.

The animal stopped in front of her and barked.

"Did you come to save me?" she asked, roughing up the hair on his head.

"We came to save you." A light bobbed down the trail toward her.

She stared beyond the bright light and recognized Ryan's shape and that of Hawke.

"What are you doing out here?" Ryan asked, putting his arms around her.

"I wasn't ready to go back in the lodge without you and thought I'd take this trail not realizing how late it was getting." She hugged him back and smiled at Hawke. "Thank you for coming to look for me. I wasn't sure if it was closer to go back or keep going."

"You are almost to the end." Hawke walked by

them and kept on going. Dog raced ahead in the beam of the flashlight.

Shandra wrapped an arm around Ryan's as they followed the State Trooper and his dog. "How did you know to look for me here?"

"Dog. Hawke had me get something of yours. The dog sniffed it, put his nose to the ground, and headed to the back of the corral. That's when I figured you went for a walk but it was getting dark."

"We'll have to make sure he gets a treat when we get back to the lodge." She lowered her voice even though Hawke had been a witness to how much Ryan shared details with her, she didn't want to get Ryan cut out of the information because he told her so much. "Could you figure out who's clothes those were in the bucket?"

"I wish I could say yes, but they were overalls."

"Like the kind Dani wears when she's working on the lodge?" Her gut tightened.

"Yes."

~*~

Shandra took a quick shower and walked quickly down the hall, hoping to duck into the room she shared with Ryan. After all that she'd seen and heard today, she didn't think she could visit with Dani and not ask questions that would let her cousin know she was their leading suspect.

Ryan grabbed her hand as she walked into the great room. "Ready for bed?"

"Yes." She smiled at Dani, Starla, Hawke, and Clive, who had finally felt well enough to come out of the bedroom. "See you all in the morning." Shandra walked into the room and was relieved when Ryan shut

165

the door behind them.

She pulled the towel on her head off and stared at her new husband. "Do you really think Dani killed Doolie because he called her names?"

"I've seen people crack for less." He put his arms around her. "We'll keep looking for answers and so will Hawke. If it's not Dani, then we'll make sure she never knows you thought she could kill someone."

"Great!" She thumped him in the chest with her fist and crawled into bed. Now her husband was making fun of her for thinking her cousin could have killed someone.

With all her worries, she dropped to sleep before Ryan had finished getting ready for bed.

She walked through the forest. The same trail as she'd been lost on tonight. But it couldn't be. The boulder where she'd found the gold was there. Someone else was digging. She couldn't tell who, only the legs of overalls could be seen as the person bent digging. Step by step, she walked closer. When she arrived at the boulder, she climbed up to the top and looked down to the other side. Doolie's body lay beside an empty hole.

The boulder under her shook.

She startled awake.

"I'm sorry. Did I wake you?" Ryan reached out and pulled her into his arms.

"It's okay. I had a dream." She retold the dream.

"We already figured whoever killed Doolie wanted the gold," Ryan said.

"But I don't think that's what the dream means." She couldn't shake the feeling they were looking at things wrong. Was the murder over the gold or was it over something different?

After Sullen and the Search and Rescue team left the next morning with Rusk, Ryan returned to the room he shared with Shandra and began writing down everything he could remember about finding the victim and the events afterwards. There had to be something that would help piece the evidence together and point a finger at the murderer.

As the facts were listed, the most likely suspect was Dani Singer. There had been multiple arguments between she and Doolie. The man had stolen items from the lodge, though Dani had said she didn't realize they were missing. And the bloody overalls looked like the type she used when doing repairs to the lodge. While all the evidence pointed to her, her actions hadn't been those of a guilty person. Far from it.

She'd offered to help in every way possible. She'd been taken hostage and hadn't shown rage or violence toward that person. She'd only showed compassion for Clive and seemed to have taken Starla in.

Shandra entered the room. "Here you are. I wondered what happened to you. I thought we could go for a horseback ride."

"That sounds good. I'm not getting anywhere with this anyway." Ryan stood and stretched. Shandra grabbed the paper and started reading.

She studied him. "Do you really think Dani killed Doolie?"

"The evidence so far suggests it."

"Everything conveniently points to Dani. But who would gain the most from Doolie's death and Dani going to jail for his murder?" Shandra didn't believe it was Dani. She was sure Grandmother would have come

to her in the dreams if it had been a family member in
trouble.

"I think we need to have a visit with Clive and
Dani." Ryan folded the paper and put it in his pocket.
"Can the ride wait?"

"If we can clear Dani, yes." Shandra opened the
bedroom door. Clive had been sitting in the great room
when she entered. He was still there in a chair, enjoying
being waited on by Starla.

"Do you feel up to some questions, Clive?"
Shandra asked, taking the chair next to him.

Ryan sat down on the arm of the chair.

"Sure. Anyone heard if Leslie is doing okay?" the
old wrangler asked.

"Last I heard they were going to release her today,
I think." Ryan put an arm around Shandra's shoulders.
"Were you and Leslie closer than her and Doolie?"

He narrowed his eyes. "What are you getting at?"

"You've asked about her a lot since she was flown
out of here."

"You live with someone for as many years as
Doolie and I have, you get to feeling like they're
family. So his wife is like your family, too. Just like
Starla here, is family. I've known her since she was
twelve. I think that's when your momma married
Doolie."

Starla nodded. "Yeah. He was nice back then. Took
us out to dinner when he came down from here in the
summer months and took us out once a month when he
was home during the winter." She frowned. "But that
only lasted a year. Then he talked Momma into coming
up here and working. I only saw them in the winter
unless I rode up with someone coming this way."

"I remember when you'd come up here in the summer time. You made a good little wrangler." Clive smiled.

"Who would get this ranch if something happened to Doolie and Dani?" Ryan asked.

Shandra glanced up at him, he'd asked the question so abruptly. He was watching Starla, not Clive.

"Before the will was read, I would have told you me. But when that lawyer said it went to Dani, Doolie had a fit and a half." Clive nodded his head.

"What about you? Weren't you upset?"

"Naw, like I told you before, it makes sense to keep it in the Singer family. It's been there so long and means so much to them that it wouldn't be right for anyone else to get it." He raised a shaking hand. "Besides. I wouldn't have been able to keep it going much longer."

Shandra patted his hand closest to her. "You're not done for yet. Once you get over this concussion, you'll be back to your old self."

"I hope so. I really would like to work here a few more summers." Clive's eyes glistened with tears.

"Starla, did your mom think your stepfather would inherit the lodge?" Ryan asked.

The young woman stared at him, chewing on her bottom lip. "She'd said a couple of times that when Doolie got this place she was going to sell it."

"That sounds like she had expected it to go to him." Shandra shifted in the chair. "Did she say anything to you about Dani when you got here?"

Starla glanced toward the hall. "Momma didn't like her. Said she was bossy and expected an old lady like herself to do more work than she should."

169

Shandra hid a grin. She'd had the notion that Leslie was lazy. "Did she make any comments about Dani getting the lodge?"

Starla fiddled with the edge of a pillow she held on her lap, her gaze averted.

She could tell the young woman didn't want to say anything else about Dani or her mother. "You said you came up a week ago. Had you seen anyone lurking around? I know you were trying to stay out of the way and not let Dani know you were here, but I'm sure you were wandering around. No one could stay cooped up in a cabin with nothing to do."

"I'd go out after Clive would finish chores and take people on rides. I'd hike or go off fishing." Starla smiled at the wrangler. "You taught me how to fish."

"I did at that." Clive smiled.

"Dani would come out and walk around a bit, but spent most of her time working inside the lodge." She shrugged. "I don't think Momma knew I was wandering around. I always made sure I was in the cabin when she brought me food."

"Was she that worried about someone seeing you?" Shandra didn't understand. She was sure Dani would have allowed the young woman to stay considering her reason for showing up here.

"I think she didn't want Doolie to see me." She shoved her longer bangs off her forehead. "He told me the last time I saw him to quit coming to my momma when I was in trouble. That I had to learn to deal with life on my own." Her eyes darkened and narrowed. "He could be nasty when he drank. That's the only way I saw him after Uncle Charlie died."

"That's true," Clive added. "He took to the bottle

really bad after that."

"But that's still no reason to have your wife scared for her child." Shandra would never side with anyone who harmed others.

"Did you see him here?" Ryan asked.

"Doolie?" Starla asked.

Ryan peered at the young woman. "Yes. Here. Before we found him."

"He'd had that argument with Dani." Starla closed her eyes. "I don't like remembering it."

"The one where she told him to leave?" Shandra urged, hoping the young woman would keep talking.

"Yes. That night. He did leave. I saw him take the mule, but I didn't care as long as he was gone." She glanced over at Clive. "I probably should have told Dani. Maybe if she'd called and reported he stole it, he'd be in jail instead of dead."

Shandra didn't think the woman showing sorrow over a man who had not been kind to her could have killed that man. Either she was a very good liar and manipulator or she was just as compassionate as she seemed.

"The day we arrived—," Ryan said, "—did you see anything?"

"I watched the airplane land. Man, is she a great pilot." The admiration for Dani reflected in the young woman's eyes.

"I was surprised at what a smooth landing it was considering I thought we were going to land in trees if not in the canyon." Shandra laughed.

"What did you see after we arrived?" Ryan continued.

Starla shoved her hair off her forehead again.

"Dani showed you around. I was afraid she was going to open cabin three and see my stuff. I shoved it under the bed when you went into the barn. Then I went out in the woods behind the cabins and waited until I saw you sitting on the porch. I knew it was getting close to lunch and Momma would be bringing me food." She thought a minute. "But she was out of breath when she brought me lunch and told me not to go outside at all the rest of the day." She glanced at Shandra then Ryan and stared at Clive. "Do you think she saw Doolie come back?"

Shandra was positive the woman knew her drunk husband was back. And he had to be meaner than ever knowing he had no way to pay the man who was following him. They just had to find a way to prove it.

Chapter Twenty-two

Ryan and Hawke had closed themselves in the radio room after dinner. Shandra knew they were anxious to see if there had been time to learn anything about the overalls they'd found.

She was going to take a different approach. Dani and Starla were in the kitchen cleaning up from the meal of sandwiches and chips. Shandra moseyed into the room.

"Do you want help working on something in the lodge?" she asked.

Dani studied her. "You know anything about repairs?"

"Until Ryan came along, Lil and I did all the repairs that weren't too large for us on the old barn and the house." She raised an eyebrow. "I know the difference between a butter knife and a spackle knife."

Dani laughed. "Wouldn't you rather spend time with your new husband?"

"He seems to prefer the company of Hawke lately." Shandra rolled her eyes.

"You do realize you married a cop, right?" Dani put the bread in the bread box. "They are on duty twenty-four-seven, even if they aren't. Just like military."

"I knew that going into the marriage. I just didn't think his job would take up our honeymoon time." She threw her hands in the air. "That's why we came here. No phones, no way to contact him, and yet, he's absorbed in a murder case."

"Sorry about that. It's a first for me." Dani started for the door. "Come on. If you want to help, you'll need to gear up."

Shandra secretly grinned. This was what she'd hoped for. To get a look at, and talk about, Dani's overalls.

They walked out of the lodge.

"Where are we going?" Shandra asked puzzled.

"To get the tools and put on coveralls." Dani opened the barn doors, and using the sunlight streaming in, walked over to a small door at the end of the tack room. "This is where we keep the tools and things we don't want guests getting into."

Hanging on hooks along the wall were two long pairs of overalls, and three average length.

"You have overalls of all sizes." She waved to the garments.

"As you can see, the long ones don't get used much. I bought them for Clive to wear when he is working on something greasy. Using that old washing machine makes it hard to get grease out of clothes."

"That makes sense. And you have three average

size because you and whoever else can wear them?" Shandra hinted.

"Yeah, I do a lot of the mechanic work on the helicopter. As you've seen, I like to wear them when I'm working in the house. Especially after ruining that pair of pants climbing around in the rafters." She walked over to a row of wooden shelves on the wall. "Grab a pair and I'll get the spackle. Since you know how to use a spackle knife you can help me fill in cracks."

Shandra grabbed the cleanest pair of overalls.

"That's strange," Dani said to herself.

"What's strange?" Shandra glanced her cousin's direction.

"I know there was another set of overalls in this box last week." Dani tapped a box on the floor with the toe of her boot.

"Why would someone take a pair out of the box when there are some hanging here?" Shandra walked over. "You're sure there was another pair in there?"

"Yes. Because I reached in and counted. There was just the one. I added it to the supply list. Up here, I don't like to run out of things. When there is one to five of something left, depending on what it is, I put it on the supply list."

"Who knows about the overalls being out here?" Shandra liked that Dani was worried about the overalls. It meant she hadn't been the one who possibly wore a pair to bludgeon Doolie.

"Me, Clive, Doolie, Leslie. I've tried to tell Leslie she'd save washing so much clothes if she'd wear a pair when she cleaned house." Dani picked up a caulking gun and tubes of caulk.

"I thought I was spackling." Shandra flipped the overalls over her arm and grasped the spackle knife in Dani's hand.

"You'll do basically the same thing going behind me as I fill in the cracks, but this is a better product for what we're doing."

"Where did you learn all of this?" Shandra asked.

"When I learned I'd inherited this and my dad told me how rundown it was, I started watching You-Tube videos and bought several magazines and books on remodeling and repairing log homes."

"That was smart. I bet it would cost a lot to have someone come and stay here to work on things." Shandra followed Dani out of the room.

She closed the door and they walked to the large barn doors. Ryan and Hawke were both headed toward the barn.

Ryan reached them first. "What do you have?"

"You were busy so I offered to help Dani with repairs. She gave me these overalls to wear." She pointed to the barn. "In the workroom there are several pairs hanging on the wall. Dani also noticed there is one missing from a box of new ones." She knew Ryan understood what she was saying. Dani wasn't the only one with access to the overalls.

Hawke stared at her. "Why didn't you just come out and ask her about the pair of overalls?"

"What pair of overalls?" Dani asked, studying Hawke.

"We found a pair in a bucket by the washing machine last night. The water tested for blood. It has also been confirmed at the State Police Forensic Lab. It matches Doolie's blood."

Dani stared at Shandra. "The whole 'I'll help you' thing was to see if I had more overalls?"

Shandra's cheeks heated. "I've been pulling for you being innocent all along, but I have to find the proof to make these two believe it."

Dani grabbed the overalls and spackle knife from her. "I can take care of my own repairs. And as for the overalls. They aren't mine. I keep the pair I wear every day hanging in my bedroom. It has to have been the new pair missing from the box. I suggest you look for the plastic wrap it came in." She marched to the lodge.

Shandra let out a long, exasperated sigh. "Every time we think we've found something that will shine on the person who killed Doolie, we hit another dead end."

"We're getting closer," Hawke said and walked on into the barn.

"What did he mean by that?" Shandra studied her husband.

"He means, Leslie was released from the hospital and even with her broken arm and broken leg she's trying to get back up here."

"I know it's not because she's conscientious about her job." Shandra started walking toward the back of the corral. "Do you have time to walk with me?"

"I do." He put his arm around her shoulders. "I'm sorry this hasn't been the best honeymoon."

"We're together. If this had happened anywhere else, I would have been taken home or left wherever we were." She laid her head on his shoulder.

"True." He kissed the top of her head. "What do you think of Starla?"

She stopped and stared into his eyes, trying to see what he was really asking. "She seems like a young woman who hasn't had the best childhood, but she has a keen perception of the world."

"We had Sullen dig into her history. She doesn't have an abusive boyfriend. Her car is parked at the trailhead. No one gave her a ride." He pushed a strand of hair off her face. "She's a chronic liar. Can't keep a job because of it and doesn't have any friends or boyfriend."

"Oh no. That means we can't believe anything she's told us." Shandra had based some of her hopes of finding the killer on what Starla had told them.

"I'm afraid not. When Leslie gets here, we'll ask her when her daughter arrived. Clive swears he didn't see her until we found her in the lodge." Ryan slid his arm off her shoulders and clasped her hand in his. They continued walking.

"Do you think she was here long enough to have stolen those items and hid them?" Shandra didn't like thinking of the young woman as a thief and murderer.

"Either that or she followed Doolie and saw him hide the items. She probably thought they were safe, then heard Doolie telling Rusk he had the money, he just had to go get it. She could have clobbered him and planned to get the items when things died down." Ryan squeezed her hand. "We may never know the whole truth. But if we can find out it was her who killed him, she should be easy to mess up during questioning."

Ryan could tell the thought of Starla being the killer was as heavy on her mind as it would have been had he told her Dani was the killer. They talked of the scenery, how they only had a few days left, and wondered how things were going back home the rest of the walk.

When they stepped out of the trees from the trail, Hawke was sitting on the porch watching them through a set of elk antlers.

"What does he say?" Shandra asked, nodding to the porch.

"He's not easy to read. He seemed gleeful earlier to think it might be Dani, not sure what that was about, but now that it's shifted to Starla, he's been watching her like a wolf watching a rabbit." Ryan wondered at Hawke's strange behavior toward the new owner of the lodge. At first, he appeared to be angry with the woman for not informing him of her uncle's death. Now that she wasn't as clear cut as the suspect, he seemed almost unhappy. Fish and Wildlife State Trooper Hawke was a strange man.

"I think he likes Dani," Shandra said quietly, before stepping up onto the porch.

Ryan studied the man. He was in his fifties, judging by the sprinkling of gray in his black hair and the crow's feet by his eyes. He was in good shape and other than the hit to the head had proven to be a good cop.

"She's in cabin three. Thought it would look suspicious if I followed her down there." Hawke glanced at him then back at the cabin.

"Any word on her mother?" Ryan had a feeling that when they got the two together the truth would come out."

"No. Lieutenant did call back and say Rusk's things all tested negative for blood and they are believing his story that he didn't kill Doolie, heard a woman's voice, and was only here trying to find out what he could get out of Dani to cover the loan he made

Doolie."

"That doesn't make sense," Shandra said, plopping into the chair beside Hawke. "Why did he knock out Clive and take Dani as a hostage if he planned to get money from her?"

"Maybe he planned to ask her family for the lodge or just the forty grand," Ryan said.

"It doesn't make sense. Did anyone ever ask Clive if Rusk said anything while he was hauling them around?" Shandra glanced from him to Hawke and back to him. "Did you?"

Hawke shook his head. "I didn't think to take a statement from him. We had Ms. Singer's word of what happened."

"Did she see Clive get struck by Rusk?" Shandra again gave them both the school teacher look.

"Do you want to go take the report while I watch the cabin?" Ryan asked Hawke.

The other man heaved himself up out of the chair. "It is my jurisdiction."

Ryan didn't say a word as Shandra stood up and followed the trooper into the lodge.

Chapter Twenty-three

Shandra wasn't the least bit shy about following Hawke into the lodge and listening in on his interview with Clive. They found the wrangler in what it appeared was his favorite chair in the great room. Starla sat on the foot stool at his feet.

Shandra wondered how the young woman had gotten out of the cabin and into the lodge without Hawke noticing. And Ryan sat out on the porch watching an empty cabin. She glanced at Hawke. His eyebrows raised, but he didn't say a thing.

Knowing what she did now about the young woman, Shandra smiled but wasn't going to fall for Starla's sad stories. Or believe for one moment that she was being nice to the old man because she felt close to him.

Hawke latched onto one of the smaller, easy to move chairs and set it on the opposite side of the stool where Starla sat, facing the wrangler. He pulled out his notebook as Shandra sat in the chair next to Clive.

Starla stared at the notebook.

"Clive, it's come to my attention no one ever took down your account of Rusk hitting you and kidnapping you and Dani." Hawke posed a pen over his pad.

The wrangler scratched his forehead. "You know, you're right. No one came and talked to me."

"Where were you when Rusk hit you?"

"I walked into the lodge to tell Dani something and BAM, the lights went out." He rubbed his head where someone, probably Dani, had put a bandage. "I woke up and that hiker was waving a gun around and telling Dani to do as he said or he'd shoot me."

"What was he telling her to do?" Hawke asked.

With her gaze on Starla, Shandra could see Hawke watching Clive.

"He told her to help me up and we were going for a walk. I told him I couldn't walk my head hurt too bad. He just hollered at me and told her to help me up or he'd put a bullet in me and only have to deal with her." He waved his hand. "You know, if I'd been clearer headed, I think I would have realized he didn't act like he knew how to handle that gun."

"What about Dani? How did she react?" Hawke continued writing before glancing up.

"She told me she'd help me and no one was going to shoot me."

Shandra couldn't take the slow pace Hawke had in questioning. "Did Rusk ever say anything about why he was taking you and Dani?"

That got her a deadly glare from the trooper.

"He was muttering about going to get his money back one way or the other. I don't know what he was talking about. But when he'd ask me which way was southwest, I kept telling him wrong and making us go in a circle. I was clear headed enough to keep us from getting too far away." He peered into Hawke's eyes. "I knew if anyone could find us it would be you."

Shandra was surprised at the red flush that darkened Hawke's high cheekbones.

"Did he mention an accomplice? Anyone who would be waiting for him or he needed to contact?" Hawke glanced at Starla, but she'd spent most of Clive's story staring at her short nibbled on nails.

"I think Dani asked if we were going to walk all the way down the mountain and he said no. He was going to fly." Clive stared at Hawke then at Shandra. "If he'd wanted to fly, he could have made Dani fly him somewhere."

Hawke looked as perplexed as the wrangler.

Shandra got up and walked into the office. Dani had a map of the wilderness on her wall. She unpinned the map and took it out to Clive. Spreading the map across the wrangler's lap she pointed to the spot that had an X on Rusk's map. "What's there?"

Clive studied the map. "That's a big, wide, open spot on a ridge."

"Big enough to land a helicopter?" she asked.

"Plenty big enough." Clive tapped the spot. "Is that where he was trying to take us?"

"I think so. But who had he contacted to pick him up?" Shandra studied Starla who was studying the map.

"He could have paid someone," Hawke said. "There are lots of pilots around who will pick people up for the right price."

"But would that person have gone along with

kidnapping?" Shandra asked.

Hawke shrugged. "There are a few who would. They are the ones who haul supplies into the marijuana growers."

"Do you think Rusk knows that kind of person?" Shandra noticed Starla had resumed nibbling on her short stubby nails.

The sound of a helicopter shot Shandra, Starla, and Hawke to their feet.

Dani walked out of the dining room. "Who would be flying in here? We don't have any guests coming." She went to the front door.

Shandra and Hawke were right behind her.

Ryan stood on the porch watching the aircraft land. Shandra bumped his elbow and motioned with her head towards Starla who had trailed them all out.

His eyes narrowed.

By the time the helicopter landed, Dani was halfway to the landing strip. Hawke was on her heels.

Shandra and Ryan remained on the porch with Starla.

The young woman stared and craned her neck as the helicopter door opened.

~*~

Hawke's hackles went up watching a man, who had been a person of interest in several of the marijuana busts he'd participated in, slip out of the pilot's side of the helicopter. He pulled something out of a storage compartment.

At the passenger side, he unfolded a wheelchair and opened the passenger door.

Now he was wondering if Charlie's death had been from natural causes. How did Leslie Lincoln know a pot grower? Had they wanted the lodge to set up a base for growing opportunities in the area? Was this the helicopter that Rusk had planned to meet?

He tucked his cynical thoughts and expression away and strode up to the newcomers. "Leslie, good to see you up and around. I'm sure Ms. Singer didn't expect you to come back and work already." He grasped the handles of the wheelchair and shoved it across the dirt and grass landing strip.

"Hey! Any chance I can get something to eat before I head back?" the pot grower asked.

Hawke shook his head, trying to maneuver the wheelchair out of the rotor wind. "The lodge is closed until further notice."

The man glared at him, shut the passenger door, and went around to the pilot's door. He climbed in and stared point blank at Hawke. He turned the rotor blades on before Hawke and his passenger were out of the wind zone.

Dani hurried over to them. "Why did you tell him we're closed?" she yelled.

He shook his head. "Tell you later."

Together they pushed the wheelchair to the lodge. He glanced up in time to see anger flit across Starla's face when she made eye contact with her mother. It appeared he needed to put the two of them together when he questioned them.

He rolled the wheelchair up to the porch.

Ryan stepped down and took the front, helping him lift the woman and chair up onto the porch.

"I'd like everyone," Hawke looked specifically at Starla, "in the dining room."

"I didn't come here to talk to you. I came to speak

to my daughter and take her home," Leslie said.

"Sorry. You showed up here and now you're at our mercy." Hawke rolled the woman into the dining room and pushed her up to an open end of the table. "Ms. Singer, would you please bring Clive in here?"

He found it interesting the helicopter hadn't piqued the man's interest.

Ryan had maneuvered Starla to a spot where she could see her mother, but they couldn't communicate. Hawke had gained respect for the man as a detective. They thought along the same lines.

Shandra took a spot across the table from Starla. When Ms. Singer and Clive arrived, they sat on the same bench as Starla. Ryan sat by his wife.

Hawke walked to the opposite end of the table from Leslie. He sat down, smiled at everyone and peered down the table at the injured woman. "Why did you really come back here?"

She glared back at him. "I told you. To get my daughter."

"Are you sure it wasn't to take care of the overalls you left soaking out by the washing machine?" he asked.

Her eyes widened a moment. "I don't know what you're talking about."

"The new pair of overalls you took from the room in the barn. The ones you had so you could kill your husband the next time he showed up." Out of the corner of his eye, he noticed Starla squirming. Was she squeamish about what her mother had done or was the mother covering for the daughter?

"We all believed," he waved his hand toward Ryan and Shandra, "that it had been an impulsive crime of passion or impulsive rage, but knowing you purposely tucked the overalls away to keep from getting your clothes dirty means it was premeditated."

The woman's mouth opened in a round circle. "I didn't kill him. There were many times I thought about it. Premeditated like you say, but I didn't kill him."

He shifted his gaze to the young woman. "Then it must have been you. Why else would your mother have come back for you? Unless she knew you killed your stepfather."

Starla smiled, peering back at him. "What if I did? He deserved it. Always saying foul things, shoving my mother around, telling me I'm not worth the shit on his shoes."

A movement across the table, caught his attention. Shandra was fidgeting as if she wanted to say something. Hawke shook his head and peered at Starla. "How did you kill him?"

"I saw him come back with that man. I went to the barn and got the suit. I put it on. The man was gone when I walked up to Doolie. He said something mean. I picked up a rock and smashed it in his head. He fell down and I threw the rock at him."

He grinned. Everyone at the table, but the young woman, knew the man had been bludgeoned with a stick. "Why do you tell lies? Why would you want to go to jail for a crime you didn't commit?"

Starla stared at him. "You said the overalls were covered in blood."

He nodded.

"Well, I took them. I killed him."

Shandra couldn't stand it any longer. "If this is your first trip here since Dani took over the lodge, how did you know where to find the overalls? Or that they were even here?"

Starla just stared at her.

Shandra held the young woman's gaze. What would make a girl say she committed murder? Unrequited love. She leaned forward, grasping one of Starla's fisted hands. "Who are you trying to save? Harris?"

Starla's eyes flickered.

"Did you come up here with him to collect money from your stepfather?" She waited a beat, knowing the young woman wouldn't crack that easily. "You can't put yourself in jail to save him. He doesn't care about you. Do you see him here trying to save you?"

"They took him away. He's in jail. He can't save me. But I can save him." Starla said, gripping Shandra's hand.

"He's not in jail." Ryan said. "They released him because there isn't enough evidence against him."

Starla's head started to shake. "He's free?"

"That's what they told us when we radioed dispatch this morning," Hawke said.

Shandra was glad he had picked up on the ploy she'd started to get the young woman to spill what she knew.

Starla turned to her mother. "Did he contact you? Did Rusk say he'd be up here to get me?"

Leslie glared at her daughter. "I don't know what you're talking about. I've never met this Rusk before."

"Momma, who's the liar now! You introduced me to him." Starla stared at her mother with disillusionment on her face.

"You knew that Rusk fellow?" Clive asked Leslie.

She glared at him. "I did not."

He glared back. "You've always had a spiteful nature. Charlie always asked Doolie what the hell he saw in you. You were colder than an iceberg and meaner than a starving wolf."

The woman's lip curled in a sneer. "From the first day I met Doolie, he said he was going to inherit this lodge. I came up here to see if it was worth as much as he said. While cleaning, I discovered it wasn't the lodge that was worth anything but many of Charlie's personal things were collectibles or historical artifacts. I waited. And then when the old coot died, he'd left everything to her." Leslie pointed the hand on her good arm at Dani. "What was I supposed to do, let her have it all when she didn't even know what all there was?"

"That's when you started stealing," Shandra said.

"I was taking what was due me for putting up with all three of these old coots for as long as I did." Leslie's face was a mosaic of disgust.

"I can't believe you were the one who stole Charlie's, well Dani's things," Clive stood up. "And here I've been sticking up for you." He stared across the table at Starla. "And you, being so nice to me. I thought it was because you had as fond a memories of you coming up here as me. But it was because you felt bad your boyfriend hit me." He slapped a hand on the table. "The hell with you both." He stepped over the bench. "I don't want to hear anymore. I thought of you like family. You've ruined my faith in human nature."

Clive shuffled out of the dining room.

"Do you want me to go after him?" Ryan asked.

Hawke shook his head. "We'll get the answers we need right here." He stared at Starla. "Did your mother fall off the horse or was she pushed over the edge by Rusk?"

Starla stared at her mother. "Did he push you? Why?"

Leslie's mouth moved as if she were trying to figure out the words to say. "That fool Doolie had told him about the gold. Doolie told him it was missing, but Dani didn't know anything about it. Rusk figured out I did. He told me if I didn't take him, he'd hurt you." One side of Leslie's mouth tipped into a smile. "I couldn't let him ruin your life. I swear, I thought he was a successful businessman when I introduced you two." She swallowed. "He told me to take him to where I hid the gold. When we got to the viewpoint, I tried to shove him over, but he was stronger and I ended up the one falling."

Shandra studied her. "He left the one horse there so it would look as if the horse had acted up and you fell off."

"I don't know what he was thinking." Leslie shook her head. "And now you say he's no longer in jail?" Her bottom lip quivered. "You have to keep Starla safe. He'll hurt her to keep me from saying what I just did."

Hawke held up a hand. "You're telling us that the man who bumbled around in the woods and got caught twice is a murderer and threatened to hurt your daughter?"

The skepticism on his face, had Shandra wondering the same thing. If Rusk was as violent as Leslie made him out to be, he was a really good actor. Or the woman sitting at the table putting the blame on Rusk was an even better one.

From the look on Starla's face, she wasn't buying

her mother's worry for her safety.

"Do you think Rusk will hurt you?" Shandra asked Starla.

The young woman shook her head. "Harris has never treated me mean. He brought me along to find his way up the mountain and to help him convince Doolie that we needed to make Dani want to sell the lodge."

"Why?" Dani asked.

"The man who brought Momma here is a grower. He wants the land and the lodge." Starla stared at her mother. "Poor Harris loaned money, this other man's money, to Doolie thinking they would get the lodge." She glanced at Dani. "When it turned out you got it, they were upset. Especially, Ray Gerard, the man flying the helicopter. He wanted to have someone kill you. But Doolie thought he could run you off, get you to sell to them."

Leslie cleared her throat and glared at her daughter.

"Yes, Momma, you were one of the impatient ones." Starla shifted her gaze to Hawke. "She's the one who killed Doolie."

"You ungrateful brat!" Leslie tried to rise up out of the wheelchair but slammed back down when her left arm and leg wouldn't hold her up.

"Tell us the truth, Starla," Dani said.

Shandra glanced at her cousin. Had she figured out the young woman had a lying problem before any of the rest of them?

Starla centered her gaze on Dani. "God's truth, this is what happened." She drew in a breath and began the story of how she and Harris had hiked in to get the money to pay off the pot grower, but Doolie said the gold was missing. She'd decided to stay and tell her mother she'd had some boyfriend trouble. Harris was going to spend the night by himself and show up the next day as a hiker and try to figure out where Dani stood on staying. She hadn't thought Harris had killed Doolie, but she knew they had met behind the bunkhouse. But when she'd snuck into the kitchen later, she saw her mother burying something in her clothes basket. When she had a chance to look, she didn't see anything that her mother would want to hide.

"When I was out walking around, I saw her put the overalls in the bucket. As soon as I saw the water, I realized what she'd done. But I knew everyone here thought Harris had killed Doolie, and he didn't want me getting involved." Her face flushed as she peered at Hawke. "I'm the one who hit you and Clive. I was trying to help Harris get away, but he is too bungling. Both times, I helped him get away. I told him to take Dani to Ray and he could figure out what to do. But Harris got lost and you caught him. I put him on your mule, thinking it would take him down the mountain." She sighed. "Harris couldn't kill anyone." She glared at her mother. "But she has the instincts of a predator and would kill to get what she wanted."

"We'll know soon enough," Hawke said. "We should have all the results from the evidence that has been sent to the state lab in a few days."

Chapter Twenty-four

Shandra stood on the porch of Charlie's Hunting Lodge. Her bag was packed and sitting beside Ryan's. It was the last day of their ten-day honeymoon. The last four had been exactly what she'd hoped for. They'd gone horseback riding, lain in meadows talking or saying nothing. She'd walked through icy cold streams barefoot and sketched so many things she'd have enough ideas for several years.

Dani walked across the distance from the airstrip. She'd pulled the plane up to the strip early to do a preflight check. She stopped by the bags on the porch. "I hope all the excitement we had around here doesn't keep you from coming back sometime."

"We'll be back. The last few days were what we'd hoped for. I'm sure there will come a time again when we need peace and quiet and time to ourselves."

Shandra scanned the area. "I have a feeling when I come back things will look a lot different."

"That's the plan. First, I have to find a cook to finish out this season. I can't do repairs and tend to the cooking and housekeeping." Dani shook her head. "I'm going to be more thorough this time and pick people I judge will be able to do the work. I was being sentimental for Doolie's sake when I kept Leslie on."

"She's where she needs to be, in jail." Shandra had felt a sense of accomplishment when a state police helicopter landed and loaded the woman into the back. Hawke had handcuffed her as soon as they figured out she was the killer. And poor Starla, thinking she was helping her boyfriend, was also taken in for assault charges. The look on Clive's face as she was taken away in handcuffs had been hard to see.

"Do you think you'll have any more trouble from the pot growers?" Shandra asked.

"I hope not. Hawke said he'd keep a close eye on things around here." A twinkle in her eye gave Shandra the impression she wouldn't mind the Fish and Wildlife State Trooper coming around more often.

"I'm sure he will." Shandra held out a hand as Ryan joined them on the porch.

"What do you say we come back here for our tenth anniversary?" he asked.

"That sounds wonderful." She squeezed his hand. "By then maybe you'll be Sheriff and won't have to be called out all the time."

He shook his head. "I'm sure you are going to keep me involved in murders for a long time with your grandmother visiting your dreams."

Murder of Ravens

A Gabriel Hawke Novel
Book 1

Chapter One

The threat of potential poachers wouldn't spoil Hawke's day. He glanced up through the pine and fir trees at the late August summer sky to appreciate the blue sky and billowy white clouds. Half a dozen shiny black ravens circled above the trees half a mile away. So much for thinking he'd come upon the poachers before they did any damage.

He and Dog, his mid-sized, wire-haired, motley mutt, had picked up the trail of two people on horseback with a pack horse at sunrise. He'd started the pursuit after finding spent cartridge rounds at a spot where they had stopped. Only poachers would be carrying rifles during bow season and following an elk trail. From the circling birds, he feared they were too late to stop an unlawful kill.

He'd used the Bear Creek Trail to patrol Goat Mountain in the Wallowa Whitman National Forest and check bow hunters for tags.

He whistled for Dog to stop.

"Easy, Dog. We're going to go slow the rest of the way." Hawke dismounted, trailing his horse and pack mule behind him. It took longer to reach the kill site by walking, but he didn't want to chance surprising a bear, wolf, cougar, or the poachers.

He picked his way through the brush, being mindful of the scraping noises from the packsaddle being caught in the limbs of young growth pines. Any other time he wouldn't have minded. The fresh pine scent from the abuse to the limbs, filled his nostrils.

Dog's tail started whipping back and forth when they were twenty feet from the area where the birds circled.

"Don't tell me you've become friends with the bears and cougars on this mountain," Hawke whispered, easing out of the thicket and into a small clearing.

A woman was bent over what appeared to be a man's body. He noted the backpack on the ground by the woman and knew why Dog's tail wagged. Biologist Marlene Zetter. She traveled this area keeping tabs on the wolf bands that had made their way to Northeast Oregon from the Northern Rocky Mountains.

"What are you doing with a body, Marlene?"

The woman in question lunged to her feet and spun to face him. Her gaze latched onto him, skimming from his cowboy boots, jeans, denim jacket, to his face under the brim of a western hat. The panic on her face disappeared as she recognized him.

"Hawke! You nearly scared ten years off my life."

Dog bounded toward the woman.

"Dog! Sit!" ordered Hawke.

The animal flopped down on his haunches, obeying

the command.

"What are you doing up here alone and leaning over a man's body?" Hawke dropped his reins and walked over to the body and woman, studying the ground and taking care to not cover any tracks.

She pointed downward. "That's what brought me here."

Hawke scanned the dusty camouflage boots, pants, jacket, orange transmitter collar around the man's neck, and unseeing eyes. He whistled. "Why does he have one of your collars?"

She shook her head. "We were doing a count in the area. Roger is up in the helicopter. He gave me quadrants for about a mile to the north, but as I worked my way that direction, I stumbled over this."

"Did you touch anything?" Hawke walked her fifteen feet back from the body.

"No. I'd just knelt beside him when you arrived." She glanced around him toward the body. "Why is he wearing a tracking collar?"

"I don't know. Stay here. I'll start my investigation." Hawke walked over to Horse, his pack mule, and retrieved a camera. "If you have radio access, notify dispatch. Tell them I have a body. We'll need the medical examiner and a retrieval team."

He didn't wait for Marlene to reply. His digital camera, radio, and cell phone were the only pieces of current technology he used when on duty as a game warden in the Eagle Cap Wilderness. Before he began documenting the area with his camera, he did a quick look for footprints. He found Marlene's. She came from a southeast direction. He noticed two sets of tracks, one of which matched the boots on the victim, that came from the northwest. The other set came to where the man lay, there were a few scuffed marks. As if the person were hesitant to view the body. A squeamish killer? He followed the set of tracks that returned to the trees and discovered the distinct shoe prints of the two saddle horses and pack horse he'd tracked all day. This was one of the men he'd been tracking.

"I didn't hear any shots. How did they get a wolf collar?" He glanced around at the ground, brush, and trees, searching for any sign of a struggle or blood.

Nothing.

Aware he'd left Marlene alone with the victim, he took photos of the impressions and hurried back to the opening.

The biologist remained in the same spot he'd left her. Her back to the victim.

"Do you know him?" Hawke asked, approaching the body and snapping pictures.

"He looks familiar, but I can't put a name to him." She held up her radio. "I contacted Roger. He's calling dispatch."

"Thanks." Hawke patted Dog on the head when he walked by. "Stay."

Once he had all the photos, he walked over to Horse and pulled evidence bags, a marker, and latex gloves from the pack. He never knew what would help in an investigation and made a thorough search around the body for anything that didn't appear to belong in the clearing. He had gathered a small collection when he crouched by the body.

A long hair clung to the victim's shoulder. It wasn't coarse like mane or tail hair. The color was close to Marlene's two-tone brown-blonde. He'd give her the benefit of the doubt that it could have fallen when she looked down, but it was evidence and went in a bag.

Hawke had come across dozens of deaths as an Oregon Fish and Wildlife State Trooper. Judging from the bulging, blood-shot eyes, red dotted face, and scratch marks on the neck where the victim had tried to take the collar off, he'd say the man had been strangled. A check of the bolts and the tightness of the collar made him wonder how someone could have wrestled with a man this size to get the collar tightened. The bolts would have had to have been in place. He mimicked the actions it would have taken to put the collar on and then tighten it. Not an easy feat on a man of the victim's size.

Yet, there was no sign of a struggle. "Accidental or on purpose?" Talking to himself was his custom from spending so many days and hours alone with his horse, mule, and dog.

"What did you say?" Marlene asked.

"Nothing."

He felt the pockets for a wallet or identification and noticed the victim's belt wasn't latched in its natural hole. It was one hole looser. Had someone else tightened his belt? Or had the belt been the murder weapon and the collar put on after the man was incapacitated? He took a photograph.

A cell phone was in the coat pocket along with a wad of tissues. These were placed in evidence bags. Rolling the body on its side, he scanned the area under the body. The ground appeared more disturbed than from a body lying on it. Tuffs of grass had been unrooted. The retrieval team would look for evidence under the body. He found a wallet in the back pocket of the man's camo pants. A quick flip revealed a driver's license. Ernest Cusack, 20456 Elm Loop, Alder, Oregon. The victim was a local.

The wallet was bagged along with coins, a pocket knife, and lip balm found in his front pockets. There didn't seem to be any other evidence to collect.

Back at the mule, he put all the evidence bags in the pack and pulled out a small tarp. He walked back to the body and placed the tarp over the victim, using rocks to hold it down.

"Now what do we do?" Marlene asked.

Hawke walked over to his horse and started unsaddling the animal. "We wait."

"You know no one is going to get up here before tomorrow." She shouldered her pack.

"Put that down. You'll have to remain until the others get here." He walked over and slipped her pack off her shoulder. "Make camp. You're staying here."

She peered up at him. "I didn't bring overnight gear."

"I'll share." He walked over to his horse.

After placing his saddle upside down on the ground under a tree and tying Jack, the horse, out on a weighted tether away from any trees, he took the pack and saddle off Horse and tethered the mule as well.

Dog settled himself on the ground between Marlene and Hawke.

"I didn't bring a lot of supplies with me." Marlene leaned her pack against a tree, using it as a backrest.

"How did you plan to get off the mountain before dark?" Hawke tossed her a package of vacuum sealed jerky. His forefathers had survived for days with pemmican, a mash of dried salmon and berries. He survived most trips on the mountain with jerky, freeze-dried meals, and granola bars.

"Roger planned to pick me up at Wade Flat." She opened the jerky. "Thanks."

"You'll have to radio him to come back for you tomorrow." Hawke studied the woman. They had met at several Fish and Wildlife public meetings where the locals voiced their concerns about the growing population of wolves in the county. Ranchers had lost cattle to the wolves, making them angry at the animal and at Fish and Wildlife.

Some had tried using the nonlethal methods biologists suggested to keep livestock safe. But the wolf was cunning. Hawke's ancestors had revered the wolf for his fur, his cunning, and how they worked as a pack to feed everyone. His ancestors also knew the consequences of too many wolves in one area. Not only did cattle get eaten, but so did deer, elk, and mountain goats, staples of the Nez Perce over a century ago.

"Roger, this is Marlene," the woman said into the large radio she held in her hand.

Garbled words crackled in the air. "Dispatch wants Hawke to call them."

"Did you hear that?" Marlene asked.

Hawke grunted and knelt by his pack. His radio was in the side with all the evidence and his forensic kit.

"Hawke won't let me leave. Meet me same time tomorrow afternoon at Wade Flat."

"Copy."

The crackling sound ended and the forest sounds settled around them again.

Hawke glanced in the sky. With the body covered, the birds had stopped circling. The rest of the night would be spent keeping the ground scavengers from destroying the body.

He turned on his radio, listened to the crackle, and held the button down. "Hawke checking in." He raised his fingers off the button and listened.

"Is the body contained?"

"Yes. I'm holding a witness until the others arrive."

"ETA for body retrieval is ten-hundred tomorrow."

"Copy." Hawke turned the radio off, replaced it in the pack, and pulled out his filtered water bottle and a plastic bottle of water he hauled around in case he came upon a dehydrated hiker or needed it for cleaning a wound when there wasn't any water available.

"Here." He tossed the plastic bottle to Marlene. "Use this to drink. Should be a small stream to the east if you want to wash up."

"I crossed it shortly before coming into the clearing." She held up the water. "Thanks, again."

He nodded and tore into his bag of jerky. The day had been spent in the saddle with only a stop to refill his water bottles and stretch his legs. He'd hoped to catch the two he'd tracked before dark. Instead, he would watch over the victim and keep an eye on his suspect.

It would be a long night.

《》《》《》

About the Author

Thank you for reading **Homicide Hideaway**. I had fun writing Shandra and Ryan's unusual honeymoon. I worked one weekend at a horse ranch in the Wallowa Mountains helping the cook. It was as remote and more primitive than I made Charlie's Hunting Lodge. It was fun remembering things about that weekend and adding them to the story to add color to the descriptions. The only way in or out was by plane, hiking, and horseback. I flew in, in the back (with the supplies) of a two seater plane. Not a fun trip for me at the time. Now, I wish I could have been in the passenger seat.

I hope you will continue to follow Shandra and Ryan's investigations as they now work together to solve murders as a married couple.

And if you were intrigued by Gabriel Hawke, check out **Murder of Ravens,** book 1 in the Gabriel Hawke series.

If you enjoyed this book, please leave a review. It is the best way to thank an author for an enjoyable read. I love to hear from fans. You can contact me through my website: www.patyjager.net
Blog: writingintothesunset.net

All my work has Western or Native American elements in them along with hints of humor and engaging characters. My husband and I raise alfalfa hay in rural eastern Oregon. Riding horses and battling rattlesnakes, I not only write the western lifestyle, I live it.

Windtree
Press

Thank you for purchasing this Windtree Press publication.
For other books of the heart, please visit our website
at www.windtreepress.com.

For questions or more information contact us
at info@windtreepress.com.

Windtree Press
www.windtreepress.com

Hillsboro, OR 97124

CPSIA information can be obtained
at www.ICGtesting.com
Printed in the USA
LVHW081914050120
642568LV00008B/144/P

9 781947 983847